A SLICE OF *Love*

ANDREW GREY

Dreamspinner Press

Published by
Dreamspinner Press
382 NE 191st Street #88329
Miami, FL 33179-3899, USA
http://www.dreamspinnerpress.com/

A Slice of Love

Cover Art by L.C. Chase http://www.lcchase.com

ISBN: 978-1-62380-078-9

Printed in the United States of America
First Edition
November 2012

eBook edition available
eBook ISBN: 978-1-62380-079-6

Readers love Andrew Grey

A Taste of Love

"…an emotional story that will have you in tears one minute, smiling and laughing the next."

—Love Romances & More

A Serving of Love

"…a compelling tale of two men who meet under less than favorable conditions and find something that is well worth the effort."

—Sensual Reads

A Helping of Love

"A Helping of Love is more than a guy meets guy, falls in love and lives happily ever after. It's about overcoming the odds, triumphing and finding the person you are meant to be, regardless of the obstacles life tosses at you."

—5 Stars and a Recommended Read—Dawn's Reading Nook

Dutch Treat

"The emotional pull was strong and the story was great It was definitely worth reading, and will become a permanent addition to my library for sure."

—Long and Short Reviews (formerly Whipped Cream Reviews)

Love Means… No Fear

"I would recommend this story to anyone looking for romance. I also found this series to be a lovely introduction to m/m erotica."

—The Romance Studio

http://www.dreamspinnerpress.com

This story is dedicated to the real "Reggie," who was denied entry to the Milton Hershey School simply because he was HIV positive. He and his family had the courage to fight and get the school's policy reversed.

CHAPTER ONE

MARCUS WILSON closed his jacket around his slight body as he walked through the dark, streetlight-lit streets of Carlisle from his small apartment toward downtown. He drank from his large travel mug of coffee, the same mug he'd carried along this same route each morning, regardless of the weather, for the past six months. Taking another gulp of the cooling but still potent brew, Marcus tried to stop the yawn that threatened, but couldn't. It was four o'clock in the morning, and he was already on his way to work. Everyone else in town was still asleep, the way normal people should be. A car passed him on the street, and Marcus watched it go by. At this time of the morning, in a small town like this, it was unusual for him to see any cars at all. There were times when he wondered why he'd even bothered to rent the apartment. He was never there, except to shower, shave, and occasionally sleep. Marcus took another swig of his coffee and turned onto Hanover Street, walking past the old courthouse, the tower with its clock all lit up to remind him it was some ungodly hour of the morning. Yawning again, he continued on his way.

Even though the sun hadn't come up yet, Marcus could already tell it was going to be a glorious late-spring day. All the trees he passed were in bloom and smelled sweet and heavenly. He knew by the time he arrived at work, he'd need to shake the petals off his jacket, but that was as close to seeing the blooms as he was going to get. If he were lucky, he'd be able to stumble home at seven or eight that evening, take a shower, and fall into bed, only to start the whole process all over again in the morning.

Marcus crossed the empty intersection at the square in the center of town and then continued walking north for another block. His store was just around the next corner, tucked in between a small clothing store and a karate studio. A Slice of Heaven had been his dream, and six months ago, he'd managed to make his dream come true. Now he was beginning to wonder if it wasn't closer to a nightmare. After unlocking the door, Marcus opened it and went inside, turning on a light as he made his way to the back room. He didn't have time to think about all his problems right now. There was bread dough to be made and set out to rise, and doughnuts to be made, and, as he checked his book, Marcus thanked the powers that be—who'd been looking out for him—he had to bake the layers for two wedding cakes to be delivered tomorrow. Granted, that meant he had to make them, but at least it was an order that would bring in a reasonable amount of money.

The first thing Marcus did was start mixing the batches of bread dough, beginning with the ones that would need the most time to rise. He also got the oven turned on and heating, because it would take a while to get up to temperature. No one else would be in for at least two hours, and he had a lot to get done. Marcus began measuring the ingredients into a mixing bowl, putting them in the right order so they would mix properly without a lot of extra coaxing from him. Once that was ready, he started the mixing process.

For almost an hour, Marcus mixed various types of dough, setting them aside to rise before they could be formed into loaves and prepared for the oven. The ones that took a long time to proof had been made up the night before, and they were now ready to go. He began loading the oven with the loaf pans, spacing them evenly before closing the oven door. Marcus set the timer and then began the next set of tasks, sipping from his mug every once in a while.

With the bread underway, Marcus started on the doughnuts. He didn't make a million varieties, just basic ones, but his were special in that they melted in your mouth. He also made them fresh and never let them get too old. Doughnuts had quickly become one of his best sellers.

Marcus heard the bell on the front door jingle and knew Angie had come in. "Morning," he called without looking up.

"Morning, Marcus. I brought you a coffee refill," she told him happily, like she did every morning. She was an absolute godsend and one of the sweetest people he'd ever met.

"Thank you," he told her, finishing up the coffee he'd brought with him and then placing the mug in the sink. "There's bread ready to go out into the store, and the doughnut batter is all ready for you." Everyone asked him what his secret ingredient was with the doughnuts, and, truth be told, it was Angie. She knew exactly how to make them perfectly each time.

"Excellent. We open in half an hour, and that will give me just enough time to get a few batches done for the early morning crowd," she said, already checking the batter and then making sure the oil in the fryer was up to temperature before getting to work.

There were certain things that would keep well for a day or so, but most of the items Marcus made were only good for twenty-four hours, so he had to be careful not to make too much. He'd also learned the rhythm of the business. First thing in the morning, his customers were after doughnuts and bread to take to work. The case needed to look good, though, because those same people would be back at lunch or in the afternoon when their sweet tooth kicked in, but only if they'd seen something that caught their eye earlier.

As it got closer to opening, Marcus checked that everything was okay for the next few minutes and then went out front to begin setting up. The cases he'd gotten for the store were basically sealed when the doors were closed to help keep his confections and baked goods from drying out. Marcus switched on the display lights and filled the cases with bread, trays of cookies, and a few of the other confectionary delights he'd made the night before. Marcus had already found a few favorites, like the cinnamon rolls that were just about to come out of the oven, as well as his chocolate brownies and dense chocolate cake.

He'd also found that he always had to have carrot cake, because he sold at least six cakes a day. But with other things, he was still trying things out to see what his customers liked.

Once the cases were up to snuff and the items he'd made the night before were all placed and looking as appealing as possible, Marcus wiped down the café tables and began setting them on the sidewalk in the shade of one of Carlisle's street trees. He left two tables inside, and once he was sure everything was clean, he hurried back inside just in time to hear his timer going off. "How are the doughnuts coming?" he asked.

"Perfect as usual," Angie answered. It was his usual question, and her usual answer. Marcus smiled as he pulled the cinnamon rolls out of the oven and set them aside to cool. In a few minutes, he could ice them and bring them out front. "I have the first batch of doughnuts ready for the case," Angie told him, and Marcus went to where she was working and lifted the neatly arranged tray of doughnuts, then carried it out front, set it in its usual prominent spot on top of the case, and placed the cover over it.

There was always a lot of work to do in a short period of time, but that was normal. Marcus had tried coming in even earlier, but it meant that he couldn't function at the end of the day, so he'd had to get more efficient in the mornings. At opening time, Angie came out from the back room, looking every bit the bakery storekeeper. "I'll get us open if you'll put the coffee on," Marcus said, and she reluctantly agreed. "I set everything up, so all you need to do is fill the pots with water and start them."

"Thank the Lord. They'll scream if they can't have the coffee exactly the way you make it," Angie told him with a smile, already filling the pots as he hurried to the back. Marcus put the petty cash in the register drawer and carried it out front, where he closed the register and set it up. Checking his watch, he smiled. It was 6:29, and they were ready to open. Marcus turned on all the lights and put out the sandwich board on the sidewalk before walking back inside and looking at his bakery from the perspective of a customer. It looked fresh and inviting, and Marcus had to admit it smelled wonderful too, sweet and warm with a touch of spice.

Angie was wiping down the cases the way she always did, and he decided that he should take advantage of what he hoped was a momentary lull and get started on the cake layers he would need. Angie could take care of things for the next hour or so. The only thing that would pull her away would be if she started running low on doughnuts, and then he would switch places with her while she made more. Marcus began weighing out the ingredients he'd need for his cake orders as he heard the bell on the front door.

Marcus had done his training at a large bakery in Philadelphia, and the head baker had drilled into him how to do things as efficiently and cost-effectively as possible. Before he'd measured out a single ingredient, he already knew what he needed to make for the entire day, and he mixed the batter he needed for everything all at once. He also checked what he already had, making sure to rotate any extra cake layers.

"Marcus?" Angie called quietly from the door. "Will we be able to complete an order for three eight-inch carrot cakes for this afternoon? She'd like to pick them up at four."

"Of course," Marcus answered, "just have her fill out the order sheet, and I'll have them ready." Marcus knew Angie didn't need to be told what to do. He also knew she was putting on a bit of a show for the customer, making them feel special because of the same-day order. Marcus stopped measuring and waited a few minutes before going out front to collect the completed order. Thanking the customer, he went back into the kitchen and adjusted the ingredient amounts, adding what he needed for the additional cakes as well as some for the store.

The bell on the front door jingled almost constantly as he got his pans ready. Once the batter was mixed, Marcus measured out enough for each size cake layer and filled the cake pans. Over the years, he'd gotten very efficient at it, and soon the layers were in the oven. Baking was what he loved to do and why he'd opened the business in the first place. Taking a break, Marcus walked to the front of the store to check on the cases and see if anything else was needed. "What happened?" Marcus asked as he peered into the half-empty cases. "It's only been an hour."

"One of the ladies came in for something to serve her guests at a luncheon party and she bought quite a bit," Angie answered with a smile, as the bell jingled on the door and she got ready to help another customer. Marcus went back into the kitchen and opened the refrigerator to pull out more of the chocolate and fruit tarts to replace what had sold. He also made a note to put together more carrot cakes. They'd already sold two—no, make that three, Marcus thought as he saw Angie carrying one back to him. "Can you write 'Happy Birthday Sarah' in pink on this cake for the customer?"

"Give me just a minute," Marcus said, completing his notes before retrieving the pastry bag of colored icing, personalizing the cake, and then returning to what he had been doing.

For the next few hours, he worked to get everything completed and ready. Angie left at noon, and he had to have everything possible done by then because he would be alone for the next few hours, until Becky came in after school. By the time noon came around, Marcus had everything out of the oven cooling, and the cases had been cleaned and filled.

"I'm heading home," Angie said from the doorway to the store before leaning in and lowering her voice. "You might want to empty the register," she added with a grin before waiting for him to take off his apron and join her out front. She said good-bye, giving Marcus a hug. "I'll see you tomorrow, sweetheart, and don't stay too late tonight," she scolded lightly before leaving the shop.

Marcus wanted to roll his eyes at her, but he didn't dare. Angie had been one of his mother's dearest friends, and when he'd opened the bakery, she had insisted on helping him. She'd put some of her own money into the business and hadn't taken a dime in six months. There was no way he could ever have made it this far without her. More customers entered the store, and he helped them. It was the lunch hour, and while he still sold pastries and doughnuts, his bread sales also picked up. He and Angie had debated making bread at first, but in a town this size, if they didn't make some of everything, they weren't going to survive.

In the afternoon, the store quieted down and Marcus used the time to inventory what he had and get a supply order ready. He was just finishing up when he heard the bell jingle. "Hey, how are my best customers?" Marcus asked as Davey and Donnie walked in, along with their older brother, Billy. Marcus guessed that the twins were about ten or so. Billy was a waiter at Café Belgie across the street, where his partner was the chef and owner.

"Good," they both answered, hurrying up to the case so they could peer inside. Marcus saw both of the boys lick their lips in delight, the way they always seemed to. "Billy brought us over for cinnamon rolls," Davey told him, and Marcus looked to Billy for confirmation.

"We need half a dozen," Billy confirmed, leaning against the counter. "How has business been?" Billy asked. "This seems to be a tough town for bakeries."

"Sales are picking up," Marcus answered without adding that he wished they'd pick up a little more. He knew it would take time for word of mouth to get going, but....

"That's really good. I sometimes get asked about you by patrons at the restaurant, and I always send them over," Billy told him while Marcus got a box and carefully placed six cinnamon rolls inside. He also reached into the cookie case and grabbed a chocolate chip cookie for each of the boys.

"Thank you," they both said before taking a bite.

"Can I get you anything else?" Marcus asked, already knowing the answer. Billy and Darryl had a full-time pastry chef who did all the desserts for their two restaurants, so they rarely bought anything other than cinnamon rolls. But Marcus had found out that Billy loved his carrot cake. "Some carrot cake?" he suggested, and Marcus saw Billy hesitate.

"Can I order one for tomorrow?" Billy asked.

"Of course," Marcus said, quickly filling out an order sheet. Then he rang up Billy's purchase, and after completing the transaction, they left the store, the boys waving good-bye.

Marcus took a deep breath and got himself a cup of coffee before checking that everything was where he needed it to be. His cake layers had cooled, and he could assemble and ice them later. His work area was clean, and everything had been prepped for what he needed to do later. Marcus took a last look around as he heard the front door open. When he came out front, he found the mail sitting on the counter and the mailman already heading for the door. "Have a good day," Marcus called just before the door closed. He saw the postman wave as he passed in front of the windows, and Marcus picked up the mail and thumbed through the pile slowly.

His mail was divided into two things: junk and bills. The junk he threw away, and the bills, well, he placed those aside for now as his stomach clenched. He knew he had to spend some time with the books that afternoon, and he needed to go through his finances carefully, but he wasn't expecting a miracle. He only had a few more months before the money he had left would be gone. There was an old joke about how to make a small fortune in the bakery business—start with a large fortune and open a bakery. Marcus stopped himself from panicking. He needed to get the books done and balance the bank statement that had also come in the mail. Then he'd know where they were. He needed additional business, somehow, and he needed it fast.

"Hi, Becky," Marcus called as Becky, his afternoon helper, walked into the store. After stowing her purse and school bag in the back, she joined him out front. Marcus gave her a rundown on what was happening before disappearing into the back room. Getting out his carrot cake layers, he put together three eight-inch cakes and skim-coated them with cream cheese icing before placing them in the refrigerator to chill. He then started on the wedding cake layers, doing the bottom layers for both before placing them in the refrigerator. Then he pulled out the carrot cakes again, iced and finished them before carrying them to the pickup portion of the refrigerator. They'd get boxed up to go later.

He then went back to work on the wedding cakes. He needed to get all the tiers built, frosted, and chilling so he could finish the construction and decorating. It took a while, but he got everything ready for final decoration and into the refrigerator.

Marcus was exhausted, and he still had the books to do. Becky came back and got the three carrot cakes, and he went out front to greet the customer. It was a woman who looked about fifty-five, dressed impeccably. "Your carrot cake is amazing. It reminds me of what my mother used to make."

"Thank you. I use only fresh ingredients, just like your mother probably did," Marcus explained.

"I'm having a party next week—could I place my order for the cake today?"

"Certainly," Marcus answered, and he got the details of what she wanted, placed the order in the file, and then thanked the customer as he walked her to the door and held it for her.

"You're quite the charmer, Mr. Wilson," Becky commented with a sly grin. "If you decide to bottle it, my boyfriend could use some, that's for sure." Becky began wiping down the tables the way she'd been taught.

Marcus smiled and returned to the kitchen. In the far corner, he'd set up a small desk, and he fished in his pocket for the keys to the file drawer. After opening it, he pulled out his ledgers, checkbook, and statements before sitting down and getting to the very unpleasant task. There was never enough money, and while he hadn't lied to Billy—business had been steadily picking up—he wasn't yet making enough money to keep from constantly dipping into his dwindling supply of cash. He entered all the bills in his ledger and balanced the business checkbook with the bank statements. The last week or so had been pretty good, business-wise, and Marcus hoped that would turn into a new normal, but it still wasn't quite enough, and Becky was the only person getting paid right now. When Marcus factored in his rent and meager expenses, he figured he had enough cash on hand for three more months.

He worked at his desk for another hour, making sure he knew everything, and trying to figure out what he could do to make everything work out, but it came down to one thing: he needed to generate more business. But could he actually handle more business? He was already working all the hours he possibly could. In order to make more, so he could sell more, he'd have to hire someone, but without the additional business, he didn't have the money to hire anyone, let alone keep himself from starving.

"Mr. Wilson, I found this on the floor," Becky said from behind him, and Marcus wiped some of the fear and desperation he was feeling off his face before turning toward her. "I think it's from the mail."

"Thank you," Marcus said as he took the brochure. "It's nearly time to close," he added, glancing at the clock.

"I have everything cleaned up, and we can probably begin removing things from the cases anytime. There are more cake orders for tomorrow. I placed them with your book, and a woman who just left wanted to book an appointment for a wedding cake," Becky told him.

"You're an amazing girl, you know that? Most sixteen-year-olds are not nearly as responsible as you," Marcus said, thankful he had good, honest, caring people to work with.

"Thank you, Mr. Wilson," she said, shifting from foot to foot.

"Is there something you wanted to ask me?" Marcus asked. He'd rarely seen her nervous about anything.

"I'd like to learn how to bake, and I was wondering if you could teach me," Becky said. "I know you need me out front, but I was hoping that if… well, maybe on Saturdays, when Gran's here too, that I could help you."

He could certainly use all the help he could get. "Why don't we give it a try on Saturday and see how it goes?" Marcus told her before closing his books and following her to the front so they could start closing up. The whole process didn't take long, and soon Marcus was saying good night to Becky and locking the door. Then he recorded the orders Becky had taken and marked the wedding cake appointment on the calendar, noting what he had to do in the morning before getting a jump on the day ahead.

Marcus managed to get one of the wedding cakes done and the other nearly finished, as well as some items made for the store, before exhaustion caught up with him. Once he'd cleaned everything up, Marcus grabbed a few papers he wanted to review at home before turning out the lights and leaving through the front door. On his way home, he dropped the day's receipts at the bank before continuing home on the slightly crisp evening. As he walked, he realized he'd dropped something. Turning around, he saw it was the brochure Becky had given him for the Harrisburg Bridal Show. He shoved it back into the papers he was carrying before continuing on.

He wasn't in a rush to get home to his empty apartment. The town square was filled with people walking or sitting on benches, enjoying the spring warmth in the evening air. Marcus would have loved to take a seat and enjoy the evening, but he still had work to do tonight so he could go back to the store in the morning and get everything done he needed to.

"Hi, Marcus," Sebastian called from across the street, and he stopped as the head waiter from Café Belgie hurried to meet him. "Are you headed home?" He and Sebastian had known each other for a while, but it was becoming neighbors that had made them friends.

"Yes. I just closed the bakery," Marcus supplied as they fell into step, heading one block south before turning onto Pomfret Street. Marcus sighed softly. He was so tired his eyes were closing as he walked. "These days are killing me. Thank goodness the bakery is closed on Sunday and Monday." He usually spent most of at least one day sleeping.

"When do you have time for yourself?" Sebastian asked, and Marcus groaned softly.

"I barely have time to shower and eat. On my days off, I plan what I'll be doing the rest of the week." Marcus yawned and covered his mouth. "I haven't had a meal with friends in six months, and don't get me started on the fact that other than customers, I haven't interacted with another man in so long I've almost forgotten what they look like. Even if I could get a date, I couldn't find the time, and if he took me to dinner, I'd fall asleep in my soup."

"It sounds like you need some help at the bakery," Sebastian observed as they approached the next corner.

"I do, but I'm in an impossible situation," Marcus explained as they crossed the street. "I need the business to grow, but that means more labor than I can afford right now. Hopefully soon I'll be able to hire some help, but right now I'm stuck." Marcus knew exactly where he was at, a catch-22 that he didn't see an easy way out of.

"You know if there's anything we can do to help, Robert and I will," Sebastian said. "He's addicted to your cinnamon rolls, and would probably issue a ruling from the bench to keep them coming." Sebastian's partner, Robert, had been elected a judge about a year ago.

"More than anything I need to bring in more business for things like my cakes and cheesecakes. I can make them in larger quantities, and they sell for an amount that really makes the effort worthwhile. I'm just not sure how to do it." They reached the steps to Sebastian's place, and Marcus stopped. "There's a market on the square, and I've thought of trying to sell things there, but then I'd be away from the store."

"I hope you work it out," Sebastian told him. "Your stuff is the best there is. Even Maureen says so, and she doesn't compliment anyone else's baked goods." He winked when he mentioned the pastry chef at Café Belgie. She'd been in the shop a few times and had seemed pleased. "I'll see you soon," Sebastian said as he unlocked his front door, and Marcus said good-bye as well before heading into his building and up the stairs to his apartment in the back.

Inside, Marcus set his papers on the small table and found something to eat. While the microwave heated his dinner, he sat at the table and went through the papers he'd brought home. Most of it was junk he threw in the trash, but the flier for the wedding show caught his eye. That would be a way to bring in extra business. He thought about it, but like everything else, there was a cost and it appeared to be rather high. Also, in order to do the show, he'd have to close the store, so he'd not only be into it for the booth rental, but would lose a day's business at the store, as well. The timer went off, and he got up, took the plastic container of stir-fry out of the microwave and brought it back to the table. He really wished he wasn't doing this on his own. That hadn't been the original business plan, but it was the way things were now. Not letting himself dwell on it, Marcus got one of those individual-serving containers of milk out of the refrigerator. While he ate, he went through the rest of the business mail as well as his own before cleaning up and heading into the living room. He turned on his television, found a channel that worked, and settled down to watch.

It felt amazingly blissful to just sit down for a few minutes. When his phone rang, Marcus nearly didn't bother answering it, but when he looked at his cell, the display read "The General," and he knew he'd better answer it. "Hi, Dad," Marcus said after pressing the connect button.

"Did you just get home from work?" his father asked without a hint of concern about the late hour. He might as well have been asking if Marcus had just finished taking out the trash.

"Yes. I was at the bakery by four this morning," he supplied, not that his father would care.

"When I took Green Beret training, we regularly spent eighteen hours a day working," his father said.

"Yeah, I know, and when you were young, you walked to school through the snow without shoes, uphill, both ways. Yeah, I get it." Marcus was feeling grumpy and not really up for his father's self-aggrandizing at this particular moment.

"Don't be smart," his father snapped.

"Did you call for a reason, or simply to harass me after I've worked for sixteen hours and need to get up early tomorrow to do it all over again?" Damn, he sounded whiny, and he hated that. He loved his job, and he loved the bakery. There were times when he wished he had a more normal life, but he'd chosen to do this and he was going to see it through. "What did you need, Dad?" Marcus added, changing his tone.

"I would like you to come to a family dinner on Sunday." That meant that Katherine, Marcus's stepmother, had invited her children over for dinner, and his father, not to be left out, planned to have his son there was well. The invitation might have been phrased politely, but it was an order and Marcus knew it. He hated these things. His stepbrothers and even one of his stepsisters were officers in various branches of the military, exactly what his father had hoped for him.

"What time?" Marcus asked, too tired to argue with him. He knew there would be hell to pay one way or another if he didn't agree, anyway, so he made it easier on himself.

"Drinks are at five with dinner at six," his father informed him in a tone that said Marcus should very well know that. "I'll see you then." His father hung up, and Marcus set the phone by the chair. After turning off the television, Marcus turned out the lights and walked to the bathroom. It was barely eight thirty, but he was exhausted and he needed to get to bed. He tossed his dirty clothes in the hamper and showered quickly before getting into his side of the bed and then turning off the light. Why he still slept on one side of the bed, Marcus wished he knew, but he did. Maybe it was his mind's way of telling him that somewhere down under the exhaustion, worry, and drive to make his business a success, there was a man who simply wanted to find someone to love and love him back. Marcus sincerely hoped he was out there, but had no idea how he was ever going to find him. Closing his eyes, he let his exhaustion take over.

CHAPTER TWO

GREGORY SOUTHLAND sat at his table sorting pills into the containers he used to remind himself what he needed to take when. It wasn't as though he took a lot of pills anymore, but he needed to think about when to take them, so he had his morning and afternoon pill containers, and he made sure he took each one almost spot on time, each and every day. His phone rang as he was finishing, and he made sure he was done before answering it. "Morning, Sebastian," Gregory said as he closed each of the containers and slipped the afternoon set into his bag. "What's up?"

"Just calling to make sure you're okay, like I do every morning," Sebastian said, and Gregory could hear the smile on his friend's face. He and Sebastian had been lovers once, but now they were the closest of friends. Gregory had cheated on Sebastian, hurting him greatly and messing up the best relationship Gregory had ever had. In some ways, he still missed having that kind of relationship with Sebastian, but his friend was as happy as could be with his partner, Robert, and Gregory had come to terms with the fact that Robert and Sebastian were better together than he and Sebastian had ever been. "Someone has to make sure you're okay." The unsaid part of that statement was that both of them sort of missed each other.

The behavior that had cost him Sebastian had also left him HIV positive, and at one point, the disease had been progressing fast. Gregory hadn't been able to work, had lost his apartment, and had had no place to go. Gregory had appealed to the one person, regardless of what he'd done to him, who he knew would help, and Sebastian had come through for him. He'd let Gregory move into a spare bedroom at his house and had taken care of him during a bout of pneumonia that his compromised immune system hadn't been able to handle.

Sebastian had a huge heart, there was no doubt about it, and so did his partner, the more than honorable Judge Robert Fortier. The two of them had accepted him into their home and lives when they had been starting their relationship, and the two of them were the best friends Gregory had ever had… ever.

"I was just setting up my pills for the week, and in half an hour I'm leaving for work," Gregory explained to Sebastian. Under Sebastian and Robert's care and watchful eyes, Gregory had gotten his strength back and had been able to get a job. They'd even rented him the room in their house until he'd gotten on his feet, and about eight months ago, he'd been able to move out and get a small apartment of his own a few blocks away. Unfortunately, a few months after he'd moved out, the company he'd been working for as a bookkeeper had laid him off, and he'd had to find another job. Sebastian and Robert had offered him the room back, but he'd declined. It was time for him to be on his own again and to try to take care of himself. He'd gotten another job and was now working as a shipping clerk for one of the local trucking companies.

"Is everything working out okay?" Sebastian asked with concern.

"Yes. The people I work with are quite nice, and my supervisor is really a great guy. His oldest son is gay and living in San Francisco, so I know I won't have any problems on that front, and the other clerks are really helpful. I think it's a nice place to work." He was still living close to the bone because what little savings he'd been able to put aside had been eaten away while he was out of work. "I'm thinking of trying to get another job, one or two evenings a week, maybe, just to bring in a little extra money so I can get caught up, but no one seems to be hiring. I thought about talking to Russ at The Acropolis to see if he needed waitstaff…." Gregory dropped as a hint.

"You can, but I think he's got a full staff right now," Sebastian offered. "I'll ask around and see what comes up."

"I know that tone," Gregory said with a smile. "You've got something cooking." He'd been around Sebastian so much he could tell when he was scheming about something.

"I might, but I don't want to get your hopes up," Sebastian told him. "So go on to work and have a good day. I have to make sure Robert is ready for work and then I have to go too. I'll call you later." Sebastian hung up, and Gregory got his bag and lunch ready before leaving his apartment and waiting on the stoop for his ride.

One of the ladies at work lived just a few blocks away, and since Gregory hadn't been able to afford a car yet, she swung by his apartment to pick him up. Her blue Toyota pulled to a stop, and Gregory pulled open the door. "Morning, Susan," he said happily as he slid into the passenger seat. "How are you?" He always tried to be pleasant even if Susan could be as prickly as hell.

"Kate's driving me crazy," she began, pulling out once Gregory had shut the door. "She's bound and determined that we should be vegans. When I asked her why, she spouted all this crap about animal rights and protecting the environment, but I think she's got this idea that being good lesbians means we should be vegan. God knows why, but there's no changing her mind. And I have to, because there's no way I can live without butter. I could see being vegetarian—I could probably live with that—but I'm not sure I can do vegan." Susan turned onto the main road and headed out to the far west side of town, to the small industrial park where the trucking company had their offices.

"I know I wouldn't want to be," Gregory agreed. "My feeling is that it has to be an individual choice based upon your beliefs and feelings. I mean, what you eat is as personal as the clothing you wear. It's your choice, and no one can make it for you." Gregory quieted and hoped he hadn't said something he shouldn't. Susan could be touchy when she wanted to be.

"That's what I told her. For Christ's sake! We've lived together this long drinking milk and eating butter!" She mimicked her conversation with Kate. "But I'm pretty much stuck, because she does all the cooking." Susan stopped at a light, banging her hands nervously against the steering wheel. She was probably in her late fifties and looked like she'd spent much of her life driving a truck. She was outspoken with her opinions and had little tact with anyone, including her boss—or "Satan's minion," as she often referred to him—but she knew her job and most everyone else's. Gregory thought she was fabulous, but if he ever told her that, she'd probably smack him on the side of the head.

They arrived at the office, and she parked in her usual spot. "Thank you," Gregory said, like he did every time she gave him a ride. "I owe you for this week's gas," Gregory said, handing her a twenty. She shoved the bill in her pocket.

"If Kate goes vegan, you won't mind if we stop at the drive-through every now and then on the way home, will you?"

Gregory smiled as they walked toward the front door. "My lips are sealed," he said, and Susan thrust the twenty back into his hand.

"Keep it. I may need it for real food and this way Kate won't know," Susan said gruffly before yanking open the front door. Gregory followed her inside and went right to his desk. He booted up his PC and organized his invoices before getting them logged and ready to be sent out.

HE spent much of his day doing the same thing over and over. It could be pretty mind-numbing, but Gregory knew what he was doing was important and his accounting-based discipline kicked in. He double-checked all his work before sending the final invoices on to mail processing. At lunch, he went into the bathroom and took his pills before carrying his lunch to the breakroom. He had a small group of people from his department that he always ate lunch with, but he hadn't been there long enough to really feel like he fit in yet. They talked about their husbands and kids while Gregory listened quietly. He didn't have anyone to talk about, so he'd never brought up his personal life much.

"Hi, June," Grace said as one of the other ladies from the department joined them. She sat in her usual spot and placed a copy of the local newspaper next to her place. "Is there anything interesting?" Grace added, pointing toward the paper.

"Nah, I'm done with it," June said and pushed it away for anyone else to read. Gregory picked it up and glanced through it, stopping at an article about Café Belgie. There was an interview with Darryl, the chef-owner, because they'd won an award for Best Fine Dining Restaurant in the area.

"I've been there," Grace said, pointing to the picture of the restaurant. "The food's great. A little pricey, but it was well worth it."

"I know them," Gregory volunteered. "The head waiter is my best friend." Gregory skimmed the rest of the article, then opened the paper to the inside page and smiled at the picture of Darryl and the rest of his staff. "They're really good people," he added, folding the paper once again, so someone else could read it. It was then that he noticed the other ladies all looking at him. "What?"

"They're gay," June said in a stage whisper, as though it were some big secret.

"Yeah… and…?" Gregory said cautiously while the others all looked at one another expectantly. He wasn't sure how his coworkers would react to him being gay. He didn't think it would matter, but after all these years, he still got an unsettled feeling in his stomach when he came out to anyone.

"And…," June prompted with an expectant grin.

Gregory picked up the paper and opened it to the page with the picture of the Café Belgie staff. "I used to date him and now he's my best friend."

June burst into a grin. "I knew it," she said, holding out her hand to Grace. "You owe me five bucks." She wriggled her fingers until Grace placed a five in her hand with a mock scowl.

"You bet on me being gay?" Gregory asked, completely confused.

"Safest bet I ever made," June crowed as she shoved the bill into her purse. "Sometimes this job can get as boring as hell, so we always have little bets going. Never more than five bucks, and it can't be anything cruel or dirty. Other than that, anything goes," June explained. "It's all in good fun and simply something to add some excitement to days of processing invoices and sending out bills."

"So, do you have a boyfriend?" Molly asked from down the table.

"Not at the moment," Gregory answered, looking around to see if more money was going to change hands, but none did, and he opened his lunch bag and pulled out his sandwich before slowly starting to eat. Sometimes the medication he was on took away his appetite, and he had to remind himself to eat regularly, regardless of whether he was hungry or not.

"Are you looking?" Molly asked. "Because I have a brother who's gay."

"Please," Grace said teasingly. "Jack is nice, but he's a little old for Gregory, don't you think?"

"I'm sort of looking, but I'll find someone on my own." Gregory wasn't sure how serious he wanted to be. All the things in his life were a little much for most people to take. In a place like New York or San Francisco, he figured he might have a chance to meet someone, but here in Carlisle, what were the chances? He figured that after Darryl and Billy, Robert and Sebastian, and Russ and Peter, all the luck in the love department had probably been wrung out of this town. Besides, he'd had a chance at love and he'd completely blown it, so he kind of figured he'd already used up his luck. "My life has been really up and down for a long time, so I need to get myself settled before I start dating. And for the record, I don't have anything against older guys, so I may get back to you about your brother." Gregory winked, and Molly smiled.

They continued talking through the rest of lunch, and Gregory managed to finish all the food he'd brought. When it was time to go back to work, he threw away his trash and walked through the office area to his small cubicle in the back. He was hard at work a few hours later when his phone rang. Checking the clock, he decided to take his afternoon break and headed to the breakroom as he answered the phone.

"Hey, Sebastian. Before you ask, I ate my entire lunch and remembered to take my pills," Gregory said, and he heard Sebastian laugh.

"Then I've trained you right and my work is done," Sebastian quipped. "Actually, I called because I may have a line on that part-time job. But it's a bit complicated, so I was wondering if we could get together at your place after work, and I'll fill you in on the situation."

"Why does this sound ominous?" Gregory asked as a few other people wandered in for coffee and then wandered out again. He usually had his afternoon decaf at his desk, as well.

"Like I said, it's complicated, and I'll explain everything tonight when I see you," Sebastian promised.

"Okay, I'll see you tonight," Gregory agreed before hanging up the phone. After filling a paper cup with decaf coffee, Gregory returned to his desk and got back to work, wondering just what Sebastian had in mind. For the life of him, Gregory couldn't figure out what was complicated about a part-time job, but he'd known Sebastian long enough to listen to what he had to say.

At the end of the day, he waited for Susan, and she drove him home. "Kate called me three times today. That woman needs more to do. Since she retired last year, she has too much time on her hands and she keeps bugging the hell out of me."

"Has she said anything more about the whole vegan thing?" Gregory asked quietly.

"God, yes," Susan answered, rolling her eyes. "This weekend she wants to bury all the animal-based food in the corner of the backyard and then hold a ceremony to cleanse the refrigerator and kitchen of all the residual animal spirits that might have lingered."

Gregory was about to laugh, but Susan was dead serious, and he had to bite his lower lip.

"What did you tell her?" Gregory asked as solemnly as he could. One thing he'd learned very early on was that Susan loved Kate dearly, so he needed to tread lightly.

Susan shook her head. "What could I say to that?" she asked loudly, braking for one of the lights. "It's a terrible thing when you have proof that the cheese of the woman you've loved for thirty years has completely fallen off her cracker."

Gregory couldn't take it any longer. He leaned forward and damn near choked, he was laughing so hard. "I'm sorry," he said as he held his stomach—but he couldn't stop himself.

"Gregory," she snapped in a tone that for a second reminded him of his father.

He straightened up and turned toward her, wondering what the fallout would be. Then she began to laugh, taking him right along with her. Susan pulled the car off to the side of the road before completely losing it. "What am I going to do?" she asked, wiping her eyes on a tissue once she'd gotten control of herself.

"Xanax?" Gregory offered. "Better living through chemistry."

"She won't take anything unless she's near death," Susan explained, calming herself down a bit.

Gregory felt a fit of giggles coming on. "Spike her tofu, she'd never know the difference," he offered, and he and Susan began to laugh all over again, until tears rolled down their cheeks.

Eventually, they got hold of themselves and Susan pulled the car back onto the road. They rode to Gregory's apartment still on the verge of laughter. She parked the car, and Gregory got out. "Good luck," he said, and Susan smiled. After saying good night, Gregory closed the door, and Susan zoomed off as Gregory pulled out his phone and called Sebastian. "I just got home."

"Okay. I'll be by in a few minutes," Sebastian said.

"Aren't you working?" Gregory asked as he walked through the front door and up the stairs to his apartment, where he unlocked his door to let himself inside.

"Yes, but everything is pretty quiet right now and we're all set up for dinner, so I can give you a while before the dinner service starts," Sebastian told him, and Gregory could hear the breeze on the phone. "On second thought, can you meet me at the restaurant and I'll fill you in?"

"Give me a few minutes and I'll walk over," Gregory answered before disconnecting the call. He ate a small snack and made sure he wasn't forgetting anything before he left the apartment and started the walk to Café Belgie.

The walk in the spring air was pleasant and helped clear his head. Gregory was still wondering just what Sebastian had in mind, but he'd find out soon enough. He arrived at the restaurant and walked inside. Billy met him and pointed him toward a table.

"Sebastian is meeting with Darryl. There's some sudden crisis that needs their attention, but he'll be right out," Billy explained, then he retrieved the coffeepot and filled a cup for Gregory. "Do you need anything to eat?"

"I'm good. Thank you," Gregory said, and Billy hurried off, returning the pot to the warmer before going to sit back where he'd been folding napkins. Gregory sipped his coffee, and, after a few minutes, Sebastian joined him at the table, carrying a plate he set in front of Gregory. "What's this?"

"Just try them," Sebastian said, handing him a fork. Gregory took it and ate a bit of the cake before tasting the cinnamon roll.

"Did Maureen make these? Because they're out of this world." Gregory continued eating the cinnamon roll, letting the frosting mix with the rich cinnamon in a near orgasmic experience. Once the cinnamon roll was gone, he ate more of the cake. "I love carrot cake," Gregory said with his mouth full. It had been a long time since he'd really had an appetite, but this was heaven.

"No, Maureen didn't make this. They're from A Slice of Heaven," Sebastian told him.

"That new bakery across the street?" Gregory motioned in the bakery's general direction before finishing off the cake.

"Yes, and that's what I wanted to talk to you about. Marcus is the owner of the shop, and he's a really nice man. He lives next door, and I sometimes hear the man going to work at four in the morning, and he doesn't come home until eight at night," Sebastian explained rather earnestly. Gregory wondered what this had to do with him, other than it seemed like Marcus needed help. "The thing is, he's in a bit of a bind. He's working and doing all he can to support his business and he can't work any more hours himself, but the business needs to grow if he's to survive. In order to grow, though, he has to hire more people… people he can't afford."

"Okay," Gregory agreed. "That sounds like a dilemma."

"And that's where you come in. He needs help with his books, because most of the time after working all those hours, he's carrying them home to work on before going to bed, and he needs someone to help free him up to do what he can to grow the business," Sebastian told him.

"Okay, I get that, but you said he didn't have the money to hire anyone," Gregory said, feeling a bit confused. "So I don't get where you're going with this."

"Okay. I'll explain it to you. After you moved out, you asked me and Robert if there was something you could do to pay him and me back for the kindness we showed you. Well, this is it. Robert and I helped you, so I want you to help Marcus. It doesn't have to be long-term, but you've tasted what he can do and you know this town desperately needs a bakery like his. He needs help with promotion and moving his business to the next level so it can prosper and grow. You know how to do that. The man is working so hard he can't plan for the future, and he needs to."

"So you want me to volunteer my time at the bakery?"

"Actually, what I want you to do is think about it," Sebastian told him, and Gregory suppressed a groan. There was no way he could say no when Sebastian made his little puppy face.

"But what I need to do is make extra money," Gregory protested without heat.

"You need to get out and become part of the real world again, to feel useful and make a difference." Sebastian stood and took away the plate as Gregory finished his coffee. "Just come with me and meet Marcus. I won't force you to do this, but at least think about it as a favor to me." Sebastian took care of the last dishes and motioned toward the door. "I'll be across the street for a little while," Sebastian told Billy, who waved at him from where he was sitting.

They walked down the sidewalk and crossed at the corner before entering the bakery. There were a few customers inside, and they waited until the young girl behind the counter had finished with them. "Is Marcus available?" Sebastian asked, and the girl walked toward the back of the store before returning quickly.

"He'll be right out," she said. "Can I get you anything while you wait? Maybe a cinnamon roll?" she asked, ready to take their order.

"No, thank you. I talked to Marcus earlier and told him we'd be by," Sebastian explained, and Gregory looked around at the cases that held the baked goods. Everything looked totally yummy, and the place smelled as good as the cinnamon roll he'd eaten earlier.

"Can I help you?" A mellow voice pulled his attention, and Gregory turned and found himself looking into the brightest blue eyes of anyone he'd ever seen. "Oh, hi, Sebastian," he said, but Gregory saw that his eyes didn't shift away from him.

"Marcus Wilson, this is Gregory Southland. He's the man I spoke to you about," Sebastian said, and Gregory noticed that Marcus wiped his hands on his apron before taking his to shake it.

"Sorry. I was working with buttercream and got some on my hands," Marcus explained, motioning them toward the back. "You were a little mysterious when you spoke to me earlier," Marcus told Sebastian as he led them through the kitchen area to his desk.

Sebastian looked at him, and Gregory knew he was expecting Gregory to make a decision. "Sebastian told me that you need some help. I have bookkeeping experience and I've worked retail and in restaurants." Gregory pulled up one of the folding chairs that Marcus indicated.

"I do need the help, but I can't afford to bring anyone on right now," Marcus said, and Gregory could hear the touch of frustration and worry in his voice.

"I'll be honest with you. Sebastian helped me out when I was sick and had no place to go. I probably would have died if it hadn't been for all the help he and Robert gave me. He did it out of the goodness of his heart, and I owe him a great deal. He asked me to come over to talk to you because you need help, and I like to eat, especially your cinnamon rolls. So, for now, you can pay me in cinnamon rolls."

Gregory saw Marcus smile, and it made him want to smile too. "I can't do that, but how about if I pay you what I can plus cinnamon rolls?"

"I need to get back to the restaurant, but you two finish talking," Sebastian said, and Gregory felt him pat his shoulder lightly before he walked out of the kitchen.

"So how much time do you think you could work?" Marcus asked.

"I could probably help a couple nights a week and part of the day on Saturday if you needed me. As I said, I know how to work in a store and I can help with the books, but I don't know anything about baking and stuff. I understand food safety, though, and…." Gregory trailed off because Marcus had begun to grin.

"Sorry, I was off in my own thoughts. During the summer, there's a market on the square on Wednesdays, and I'd really like to have a booth there a couple of times. I don't want to sell anything, but I thought we could give away samples to get people into the store. The heat isn't good for baked goods, and a lot of what I sell has butter in it, but I'm hoping samples will translate into people walking the block to the store to shop."

"I can do that, I think. I know how to cut cake and stuff," Gregory said. "So since today's Thursday, do you want me to start tomorrow evening? I get off work at four and can be here about four thirty." What surprised Gregory was the excitement that flowed through him. This could be really interesting, and it might even turn out to be fun. It wasn't as though he was committing to a great deal of time or anything.

Marcus appeared surprised. "Okay. Maybe we can review the books and you can help make sure I have everything right. Then I'll train you how to run the register and help with the customers," Marcus told him, and Gregory saw some of the worry slip from Marcus's expressive handsome face. Sebastian had told him that Marcus was trying to do everything, so maybe a little help really was what he needed.

"There's one more thing: I'm HIV positive," Gregory said honestly. "It isn't a problem for me to work in food service as long as I'm not experiencing symptoms, and I'd wear gloves whenever I handled food anyway, but I thought you should know. If you don't want me to work here, I'll understand."

Marcus shook his head. "I had a friend who died not too long ago of the complications from HIV. I'm not sure if he was one of the lucky ones or not. He died very suddenly. He caught a virus that his body couldn't fight, and it went straight to his heart. That was about a year ago, I guess. Teddy and I had planned to open the bakery together, but he didn't make it."

"Were you and he lovers?" Gregory asked, and Marcus shook his head.

"I'm not sure what we were. I mean, we'd had sex, but our relationship was different. Teddy needed care, and his family had pretty much abandoned him, so he moved in with me and we shared a bed. We had sex a few times, but our relationship wasn't about that as much as it was the closest friendship I've ever had in my life." Marcus looked away, and Gregory sat silently, willing to listen. "When we met, he was already positive and on all kinds of meds. He got better for a while, and we made plans to open the bakery. He was going to run the front and handle the business side of things, and I was going to bake. That was the plan, anyway."

"So you went ahead with the bakery?" Gregory asked, a bit surprised that Marcus was opening up to him this way, but maybe it was the knowledge of a shared pain.

"Yeah. Teddy left me his portion of the business, and I couldn't walk away from the dream—it would have been too much like walking away from Teddy. It's been hard, but I don't regret it." Marcus sighed very softly. "Sorry, I shouldn't have dumped my sad story on you. I mean, we only met a few minutes ago."

"It's okay. Maybe over a cinnamon roll I can tell you my own sad story sometime, although mine sounds a lot like Teddy's," Gregory said before standing up. "I know you have work to do and I don't want to keep you, but I'll see you tomorrow at four thirty." Gregory shook Marcus's hand, holding it longer than necessary, because while slightly rough, his skin felt nice. "Night," he said, and he walked out to the front, where he stopped to peer into the case. "Would it be possible to get one of those carrot cakes?" he asked. "I'd like to take it into work tomorrow."

"Of course," the cashier said before taking the cake out of the case and placing it in a bakery box. Gregory paid for it and carried it out with him on his walk home. This had promise. Marcus seemed nice, and he could earn a little extra money. Not as much as he hoped, but he felt good about what he'd decided to do. Besides, Marcus was… well… adorably cute. Not that he had any real hopes, and after what he'd done to Sebastian, he wasn't sure he deserved any.

CHAPTER THREE

MARCUS stayed exceptionally busy. Fridays were usually good days for orders and for people picking up their cakes, but today seemed especially busy, and Marcus couldn't help wondering if this was a sign of things to come. God, he certainly hoped so, and if Gregory worked out and got along with the rest of his team, things might just be looking up. Being this busy also meant that by the time Angie left, he still hadn't finished all of the work he needed to complete. So he spent much of the afternoon working in the kitchen while he listened for the bell at the door. He got a number of cakes put together because he did have lull times, but he was exhausted. He'd been going on complete overdrive all day, and when he saw Becky walk through the front door, he wanted to hurry around the counter and hug her.

"The store has been really busy, Becky," he told her. "I'm sorry I haven't been able to keep it as clean as usual, but I've been running back and forth between the store and kitchen all afternoon." Marcus had stressed to both Angie and Becky the importance of keeping the store as spotless as possible, and he hated that he hadn't been able to lead by example today.

"It's okay," she told him with a smile.

He wasn't so sure, but he was grateful for her attitude. "There are a dozen items ready for pickup and I have more to complete for tomorrow morning." Marcus headed back to the kitchen as Becky signed in and got to work. "Oh," Marcus said, shaking his head. "We have a new person starting this evening. His name's Gregory, and if you can show him around the store and teach him what he needs to know, then tomorrow, after he comes in, you can work with me in the kitchen and we'll see what you can do."

That got a grin from Becky. "Thank you," she said and bounded to get her cloth and start wiping up. Marcus watched her and remembered that happy feeling the first time he'd been told he was going to be given a chance. Granted, that euphoria usually wore off pretty quickly, because the job wasn't as glamorous as many people thought it was.

"Call me if you need me," he told Becky before returning to the kitchen to get to work. He'd just placed another completed order in the refrigerator when he saw Gregory standing in the doorway.

"Sorry, I didn't want to disturb you," Gregory explained.

"No problem," Marcus said, wiping his hands. "I put together the papers you need to complete, and then I thought you could work with Becky to learn what we do in the store. I'm hoping that you could spell her in the store so she can help me in the kitchen for part of the day tomorrow."

Gregory smiled at him, and Marcus felt his pulse speed up just a little bit. He'd had a similar reaction yesterday when they'd been talking. Marcus cringed inside as he remembered the things he'd told Gregory. The man must think he was a real sad sack to have told him all that stuff right after meeting him. Marcus led Gregory toward his desk and handed him a small stack of papers. "I'm sorry about yesterday," he said softly.

"What for?" Gregory asked.

"All that stuff I sort of dumped on you," Marcus said. He usually didn't talk about his personal life like that with people he'd just met.

"It's okay. We've both been through the same thing, just from different angles. Sometimes it's good to talk about it. Besides, someday I'll probably tell you my own story, and then we'll be even, trust me." Gregory smiled, and it was like a light came on in his deep brown eyes. Marcus had been about to explain the forms he needed Gregory to fill out, but his mouth had gone dry and the words he'd been about to say flew from his head. He had to take a breath and think for a few seconds, but nothing seemed to come. All he could concentrate on were Gregory's eyes and his full lips. He had to get it together.

"These shouldn't take long," Marcus stammered, indicating the forms.

Gregory pulled out the desk chair and sat down. "Just let me know when you're done and I'll introduce you to Becky." God, he felt like an idiot. He couldn't even give basic instructions. Marcus knew he was a little nervous and kind of excited, but with his stammering and empty-headedness he felt like a bit of an airhead, and he wondered what Gregory must be thinking.

"I will," Gregory told him and began filling out the papers. Marcus watched him for a few seconds, taking in how slight he was, but there was a glow to his skin, and Gregory's dark-blond hair looked bright and shiny. Swallowing hard, Marcus moved away, backing into one of the worktables, and it scooted on the floor. Turning away so Gregory wouldn't see him blush, Marcus went back over to where he'd been finishing cakes and got to work.

He got almost nothing done. Between each step, Marcus found himself stopping to look over at Gregory. He couldn't figure out what was so fascinating about him, but if he didn't get his head where it belonged, along with other things, he wasn't going to get his work done and he'd be behind for tomorrow. Forcing his attention back to his work, he finished the last of the cake orders for Saturday and began cleaning up his workstation.

When he looked back at the desk, he saw Gregory get up and walk through the kitchen toward the store. He made to follow, but Marcus could already hear introductions and then Becky explaining to Gregory how things worked. After a few minutes, they both walked to the order cooler, where she got out two cakes and told him what they did and how they packaged them. Knowing Gregory was in good hands, Marcus started the batches of dough for the slow-rising breads to get them ready for the morning. He wanted to hope that things were getting better and that there was light at the end of the tunnel, but he didn't dare, not yet anyway.

Once he'd finished the dough and had it set to ferment overnight, he cleaned up again and got ready to close up the kitchen for the night. "Marcus," Gregory called from the kitchen doorway. "There's someone out here you need to speak to." Marcus looked up from what he was doing as Gregory walked toward him. "Becky asked me to come get you."

Marcus wiped his hands, then set aside his cloth and walked out to the store. He saw a young couple sitting at one of the tables. The man was obviously comforting an attractive young woman, who was very near tears. "Can I help you?"

"This is Julia and her fiancé Rafael," Gregory told him.

"What can I help you with?" Marcus asked.

"We're supposed to get married on Sunday, and the bakery that was supposed to make our cake lost our order." She broke into sobs.

"It's okay, Julia," Gregory said. "If Marcus can help you, he will."

She sniffled a few times, and Rafael stood, lightly patting her shoulder. "The bakery that was supposed to do the cake put down the wrong date for our wedding," he explained with a slight accent. "We called to confirm a little over a week ago, and they somehow messed up between then and now. We'll have four hundred people on Sunday and no wedding cake." To Marcus's surprise, Rafael looked at Gregory. "Julia works with Gregory at the trucking company, and he brought in a cake today that she said was fantastic, and he told everyone where he'd gotten it. We were hoping you could help us." Rafael looked like he'd given up hope, and Julia looked about to cry again. But it was when Marcus saw the way Gregory was biting his lower lip, looking almost as nervous as the bridal couple did, that he decided he had to give it a try.

"What did you have in mind?" Marcus asked. A cake for four hundred people was going to be a massive amount of work.

Julia reached into her handbag and pulled out the order sheet from a bakery in Mechanicsburg. Marcus read it over and shook his head. The cake they'd ordered would require hours of piping and icing work that there simply wasn't time to do. "I can't do this cake," Marcus began, and he saw both of their faces fall. "I don't have the time to do all this work." Marcus pulled over a chair from the other table. "But if we simplify it a little, you can have a gorgeous cake."

The bride and groom both relaxed, and Gregory stepped away from the table.

"The basket-weave pattern on the layers is a beautiful effect, but it takes more time than we have. Do you have a picture of your dress?" Marcus asked, and Julia nodded, pulling a photo out of her handbag. "This is beautiful and you're going to be stunning in it." Marcus studied the picture for a few seconds. "How about instead of the basket weave, we pipe pearl swags on the cake to mimic this detail on your dress. It'll make the cake design clean and more elegant. I also suggest that instead of the gum-paste flowers, you use real flowers." Marcus continued reviewing the order. "The rest I think I can do for you." God, this was going to be a massive amount of work.

"You can?" Julia asked, her tears drying for the first time since he'd seen her.

"Yes. Let me write up the order." Marcus stood and got the order pad. "There's just one more thing. We aren't open on Sunday. Is there someplace we can deliver the cake late tomorrow?"

Rafael nodded and explained where the wedding was being held. "We had made arrangements for Saturday delivery from the other bakery, and the hall will be open late on Saturday because there will be another wedding going on."

"Okay," Marcus said as he completed the form, making note of all the details they'd changed, as well as the venue, and finally, he took a few minutes to compute the cost. Because of the simplifications and adding a slight premium for the rush order, he still brought the cake in at under the price quoted by the other bakery, but not by much.

They seemed thrilled anyway, and Rafael signed the order and wrote him a check for the cake right on the spot. Both of them stood, and Julia had a smile on her face for the first time. "Thank you for saving our wedding," she told him.

"You're welcome. I'll call if there are any more questions," he said, and he walked the now happy couple to the door. Once it closed behind them, Marcus took a deep breath and then let it out, trying to clear his swimming mind. The bill for that cake alone was as much as the store usually took in for two whole days.

"Is there anything we can do to help?" Becky asked from behind the counter.

"Yes. Can the two of you close up alone?" he asked, and Becky nodded with an "of course" type of expression. "I've got to check that I've got the ingredients I need." Marcus started heading into the kitchen almost before he'd finished speaking. He spent nearly half an hour writing up all the details for what he'd need—the cake, the amount of buttercream, as well as fillings. Then he put together the list of ingredients and checked it against what he had. *Just enough* was the answer. He'd have to go to the store after closing to make sure he had enough eggs and butter on hand for tomorrow, but he could do it.

"The store is closed and all you need to do is take care of the register," Becky told him from the doorway. "Do you need me to stay and help you?"

Marcus shook his head. "No, but come in early tomorrow and you can help me in the back. There's going to be a lot to do here, and Gregory," he said as he lifted his eyes to where Gregory stood behind Becky, "can work out front with Angie." Marcus hardly knew what he was going to do with actual help in the kitchen. He hadn't had any, other than Angie making the doughnuts in the morning.

"Really?" she asked with delight.

"Yes. So wear dark pants and a white shirt. They need to be clean, but they probably won't stay that way," he told her before adding, "See you in the morning."

She hurried away, and Marcus heard the front door jingle as she left. He walked up front and locked the door before removing the cash drawer from the register and carrying it back to the office area. "Do you need to leave?" he asked Gregory as he emptied the cash drawer and put the money in the safe hidden in the wall under his desk.

"I can help you if you want," Gregory offered. "I know you have a lot of work to do because of that wedding cake order."

Marcus smiled as he nodded. "The one you got for me," Marcus said with a grin. "If you hadn't taken that cake in to work and told everyone where you got it, they wouldn't have known about us, so thank you. And I won't turn down the help." Marcus checked that everything was all buttoned up before stepping to his work area. "I know you don't know much about baking, but you can help anyway." He pointed to the paper on the table. "Please get the refrigerated ingredients for me. Be sure to take what's in front first."

Gregory looked at the paper and then began gathering the items while Marcus started measuring the dry ingredients into the large mixer. When he was shopping for the bakery equipment, he'd wanted a large stand mixer, but they were so expensive he didn't feel he could afford one. When an old department store in Harrisburg had closed a month before the bakery opened, he'd gone to the closeout sale and bought his forty-quart mixer for a song, and, boy, was he happy he had it today. Marcus knew he'd gotten the bakery deal of the century. Once the dry ingredients were weighed, Marcus began measuring out the liquid ingredients. "Can you crack eggs?" Marcus asked Gregory as he got him a bowl and large measuring containers.

"When I was a kid, cracking the eggs for Mom's cakes was something I did all the time," Gregory told him, and he began cracking the eggs into a bowl as Marcus got the butter softening in the microwave.

"Be sure to watch for any bits of shell. Nothing ruins a wedding for a guest as fast as a bit of crunch in their cake."

"I'll remember that," Gregory said as he continued carefully breaking the shells, peering constantly into the bowl. The microwave beeped, and Marcus added the butter to the mixer, scraping the bowl clean with a scraper. Once Gregory was done cracking the eggs, Marcus poured them into a measuring cup, checking for shells as he poured. He also got milk and vanilla, measuring these as well.

"Start getting out the pans, please," Marcus instructed. "I have the sizes we need listed on the sheet." He helped Gregory get down the pans and set them out on the worktable. He then showed Gregory how to grease the pans and line the bottoms with parchment paper circles. Once they were ready, Marcus turned on the mixer and slowly added milk as the ingredients blended. Marcus continued mixing, adding the eggs and flavorings. Once the batter was ready, Marcus turned off the mixer and lifted out the paddle, then scraped down the sides before giving the batter one final mix. Then he lifted out the paddle again, scraped it down, and placed it in the sink.

Together, they filled the pans, using a scale to determine the proper portion for each. Then he got all the pans loaded into the oven and closed the door. "Now they just need to bake?" Gregory asked.

"Yup. I need to get the basic components of the buttercream and fillings ready. Do you think you could wash the mixing bowl and other things for me?" Marcus watched Gregory move. "You aren't too tired, are you?" Marcus remembered how often Teddy had been.

"I'm fine," Gregory answered, but Marcus got a couple doughnuts and put them on a plate, setting it near where Gregory was working. "What do you do with the leftovers?"

"If it doesn't have icing on it, I grind it up and dry it to make cheesecake crusts. If it has icing on it, I keep it refrigerated and use a food processor to turn it into cake truffles or filling for special pastries. Nothing goes to waste or I'd never be able to make any money," Marcus explained as he got the ingredients together for the buttercream, and when Gregory finished with the mixing bowl, he checked it over out of habit and then began the basic mixing process. Once that was done, he divided the icing into manageable amounts and put it in the refrigerator. Gregory washed the bowl again while Marcus made sure he had the flavorings he needed. By the time he was done, the cake layers were ready to come out of the oven, and once he got the layers on the racks to cool, they were done for the evening. Gregory had finished doing the dishes, and Marcus wiped all the work surfaces before checking the bread batches one last time.

"We're done?" Gregory asked, and Marcus nodded.

"Yes. Are you hungry? Because I'm starved, and I'd say we earned dinner." Marcus took off his apron and placed it in the bag of dirty laundry he needed to take home.

"I could eat," Gregory said tentatively, looking like he was trying to stifle a yawn.

"Then how about steak frites at Café Belgie? You deserve it." Marcus looked everything over one last time before he turned out the lights and headed to the front door, with Gregory following him. He was exhausted, but keyed up. It looked as though he was going to actually finish the wedding cake on time. He opened the door and let them out before locking the door behind them.

Gregory walked toward the corner, and the light changed, allowing them to cross the street. Marcus found himself hanging back a little, and his gaze wandered to where Gregory's round little butt bounced in his black khakis. He tried not to be too obvious, but it was hard to tear his eyes away. As they approached the restaurant, Marcus waited as Gregory opened the door, and then they walked inside.

"Are we too late for dinner?" Marcus asked Sebastian as he walked through the dining room.

"We were just about to close. I'll see if Darryl still has the grill on," Sebastian said, hurrying away. "What do you want?" he asked just before disappearing into the kitchen.

"Steak frites," Marcus said, looking at Gregory, who nodded his agreement. Sebastian disappeared, and they sat at one of the tables near the kitchen. The other tables had been set up for the morning, and Marcus knew that this table was the one the staff used when there weren't customers, so it was most likely the last one to be set up for the next service.

Sebastian came back out of the kitchen. "Darryl has your dinners on," he told them before walking over to the serving station and then returning with the coffeepot. "I know what both of you want," Sebastian said, and he poured three cups before setting the pot on a napkin on the table and sliding in next to Gregory. "So how'd it go?"

"Good," Gregory answered.

"More than good," Marcus interrupted. "Gregory got me a huge wedding cake order, which is why we're here so late. It's a rush job for four hundred people for Sunday, and they've already paid for it." Marcus was so excited he thought he was going to burst. This order alone was going to bulk up his cash reserves for almost a month.

"How'd you do that?" Sebastian asked.

"Purely by accident. I took a carrot cake to work to try to make Susan feel better about her partner making them go vegan, and I shared the cake with everyone else. The bride's bakery screwed her over, and she and her fiancé came to Marcus's bakery and placed the order with him. It's not as if I did anything special."

Marcus put down his coffee cup and leaned across the table. "There are going to be four hundred people at that wedding eating my cake. And I bet Julia has tons of friends her age, and every one of them is going to ask where she got her cake, because not only is it going to look nice, but it'll taste amazing. And she's going to tell everyone who'll listen about how A Slice of Heaven helped her out and how that other bakery screwed her over." Marcus could almost hear those conversations during the reception. "And that's all because you told anyone at work who would listen about the bakery. That's how word of mouth works."

"Do you really think you'll get more business because of it?" Gregory asked, and Marcus nodded.

"A four-hundred-person wedding is huge exposure," Sebastian explained to Gregory. "Catering, cake, DJ—all of them want to make a good impression because there will be dozens of potential brides attending as guests." Sebastian stood and went into the kitchen, returning with their orders a few minutes later. "I need to get closed up, but enjoy your dinners." Sebastian hurried away and got busy while Marcus and Gregory dug in.

"What time do you want me to come in tomorrow?" Gregory asked between bites of his steak.

"About eight would be good. Angie usually handles the mornings, but the shop is busiest between about nine and two on a Saturday."

"Okay, I can certainly do that," Gregory agreed between bites. They were both hungry and concentrated on eating for a while with very little conversation, but Marcus watched Gregory closely, taking in the way he groaned very softly when he got a bite of something really good. "I don't usually eat like this," Gregory explained.

"Me either. I'm usually trying to figure out how to keep myself going for the least amount of money possible, because if I'm paying to eat, then that's money I don't have for buying supplies, or paying Becky."

"Would your family help if you asked?" Gregory asked, watching as Marcus thought about his answer for a while.

"I really don't know, and I have no intention of finding out," Marcus said. "My father tends to be a very take-charge, 'you make your own opportunities' sort of man. I'm his only child, but my stepmother has three sons and two daughters. All of them seem to be on his wavelength." Marcus ate some of his fries, dipping them into the homemade mayonnaise that Sebastian had included.

"How so?" Gregory asked after swallowing, and Marcus saw a cloud pass over his expression for just a few seconds.

"My dad is a retired army general, and he always thought I would be General Junior. But to his everlasting shame, I showed no interest, and when he actually pressed me to enlist, I told him I was going to cooking school. He nearly came unglued. Not only wasn't I following in his footsteps, but I wanted to be something he saw as girlie. Thankfully, my mother supported me to the hilt." Marcus smiled when he mentioned her. "She and The General divorced when I was ten, and I always thought it was because she was the one person who didn't take his crap and would stand up to him toe to toe."

"So he and his stepkids really get along?" Gregory asked sadly, and Marcus knew there was a story there.

"Yeah. I suppose he got lucky that way. My oldest stepbrother, Hugo, is a first lieutenant in the army, and The General's so proud. The other two are in the navy. He's still so proud of them he could bust. My oldest stepsister recently graduated top of her class from West Point, and she's going to be an officer as well." Marcus drank some of his coffee and sighed. "It's not that going into the military is bad or anything, but to my father it's the military or nothing. The only exception is Eileen. She's the youngest and has my father wrapped around her little finger. She's still in college and can do no wrong as far as The General is concerned." It really hurt that no matter how hard he worked, he knew his father still looked on him as a disappointment. "To make matters worse, by some miracle, everyone is actually in town this weekend, so The General has commanded that everyone be present for dinner on Sunday." He hated those dinners. His stepbrothers and sisters were fine in small groups, but when they were all together, Marcus felt a bit like a stranger in his own family.

"At least you have a family," Gregory whispered almost under his breath, and Marcus felt his eyes widen in curiosity.

"Did they die?" Marcus asked, wondering what could be causing the loss he read in Gregory's expression.

"No. They're very much alive as far as I know. My family never understood and barely tolerated the fact that I was gay. When I was a kid, they were relatively normal, but in the last decade, they've gotten involved with a very fundamentalist, almost radical church in a big way. They could deal with me as long as I was quiet and didn't talk about my life." Gregory set down his knife and fork, his expression blank. "When I got sick and couldn't work, I called them, begging for help. I was homeless and sleeping in the car I had at the time. I barely had any energy and was praying to die." Gregory clamped his eyes closed, and Marcus could tell this was hard for him to talk about. "My own father told me he wasn't going to help me because he didn't want to interfere with God's punishment."

"Oh my God," Marcus whispered in total shock. "Just like what Teddy's family did to him."

Gregory nodded. "I haven't spoken to them since, and afterwards, I called the only person I could think of," Gregory explained, and Marcus saw Sebastian slip into the booth and place an arm around Gregory's shoulder, and for a second Marcus felt a tug of jealousy as he wondered what it would feel like to hold Gregory. Blinking a few times, he willed the loneliness that suddenly welled inside him away. It had been a long time since he'd been touched or held with care.

"Hey, you know you're part of our family," Sebastian reminded him, and Gregory nodded.

"Sebastian took me in, and a few days later I got so sick that if he and Robert hadn't been there, I probably would have died. Even after what I'd done to him...."

"Hey," Sebastian interjected. "You made a mistake; we all do. But it worked out for the best. I found Robert, and we're better friends than we were boyfriends." Reading between the lines, Marcus could figure out what had happened. "Eat your dinner," Sebastian said, and Gregory rolled his eyes, but he picked up his knife and fork and began to eat once again. Sebastian stuck around for a few minutes before leaving the booth and returning to work.

"I never gave much thought to the fact that I might be the lucky one. Although if you meet The General, you'll probably wish you hadn't," Marcus commented, and he saw Gregory smile. "He somehow manages to make every question or request sound like a do-or-die order."

Gregory swallowed, and the expression in his eyes shifted with just a touch of mirth. "So if he comes in the bakery, should I salute?"

Marcus couldn't help scoffing. "He'd never set foot in the bakery. He might send my stepmother, Katherine, to perform some recon work, but he'd just as soon ignore what I do completely." Marcus could feel the anger begin to rise the way it usually did when he thought of his father. "He's so big on respect. You'd think he'd learn to respect other people's decisions, but he only does if the decisions were the same ones he'd make. Everything else is wrong." Marcus finished the last of his food and drank his coffee while Gregory continued eating. He was tired, but relaxed, and he'd gotten enough done that he could probably sleep in an extra hour in the morning.

Gregory ate more slowly, but eventually finished his food, looking full and satisfied. Sebastian came by and took away their dishes, and Marcus handed him his credit card. "I should pay my share," Gregory said, reaching for his wallet.

"No. It's my treat," Marcus said, and he meant it. He'd gotten that cake order because of Gregory, and Gregory had helped him get everything made and baked so he could deliver it on time. "You were a huge help." He'd probably still be at the bakery trying to finish if Gregory hadn't stayed with him. Sebastian brought the slip, and Marcus signed it.

Darryl wandered out of the kitchen, and they all talked for a few minutes before saying good night. Marcus and Gregory left, both of them walking down the sidewalk toward the south side of town. When Marcus turned onto Pomfret Street, Gregory did the same, and soon he found himself in front of the door to his building. "Do you have far to go?" Marcus asked as he fished his keys out of his pocket, stepping up onto the first step.

"About a block," Gregory answered, but he didn't move away. Marcus didn't turn away either. He saw Gregory tilt his head slightly, like he wanted to ask something, but wasn't sure he should.

"What is it?" Marcus asked softly as the spring breeze rustled the leaves of the tree above their heads.

"Nothing, I guess," Gregory said, but he still didn't look away.

Marcus stepped back down to the sidewalk, intently gazing into Gregory's eyes and seeing him look right back. He stepped closer, and, pleased that Gregory didn't back away, Marcus leaned still closer and lightly kissed Gregory on his soft lips. "Thank you," Marcus said softly, and Gregory seemed surprised. For a few seconds, Marcus thought he'd read the situation wrong and he could feel his cheeks begin to warm in embarrassment, but then Gregory smiled, wide and bright, and Marcus knew he'd been right. "I'll see you tomorrow morning," Marcus said, and Gregory nodded slowly before walking down the sidewalk. Marcus watched him leave, and he couldn't be sure, but from the back it looked as though Gregory might have touched his lips with his fingers as he walked.

CHAPTER FOUR

GREGORY walked under an umbrella from his apartment to the bakery. It was more drippy than rainy, but he didn't want to take the chance that when it was time to go home it would have turned into a downpour. The bakery door jingled as he pulled it open, and he lowered his umbrella as an older woman, most likely the Angie Marcus had told him about, followed him from behind the counter with her eyes. "Good morning," he said brightly. "I'm Gregory." He continued through to the back and put his umbrella near Marcus's desk, watching as he worked with a cake, spinning it on a turntable, smoothing the icing in one clean movement. Becky stood at one of the other tables, working as well.

He continued watching Marcus for a minute before he tore his eyes away and walked back toward the front of the store. Gregory didn't want to disturb Marcus's work, but he wanted to ask him about last night. He hadn't been able to stop thinking about that kiss, and he sort of wondered if there might be another one in his future. Of course, it could have been a momentary lapse of judgment and maybe Marcus regretted doing it. He looked back in the kitchen one more time as Marcus hustled to the refrigerator, placed the cake inside, and got out a larger one. Gregory knew the minute Marcus saw him because he smiled, and the nervousness Gregory had been feeling ever since he'd walked home from Marcus's house the night before dissipated like fog on a summer morning. Gregory smiled back and then hurried out front to get to work.

"Marcus wanted me to help you out here this morning," Gregory said as he stepped behind the counter.

"I'm Angie, and it's nice to have you working with us," she said pleasantly. "Marcus told me that you worked with Becky last night. So you probably already know the routine." The bell on the front door jingled as it opened, and Angie motioned for him to help the customer.

Gregory greeted the customer pleasantly, and she stared at the cases for a long time before telling him what she wanted. He got a box, put on a pair of gloves, and filled the order. "Would you like anything else? Our cinnamon rolls are mouth-watering." Gregory waited for a second, and the woman looked at the rolls and then added two to her order. Gregory then closed the box and rang up the sale. More customers had come into the shop, so after thanking the woman and handing her the box, he helped the next person in line.

Business was fairly steady for two hours. Gregory up-sold the cinnamon rolls until they were gone and then switched to the carrot cake. He noticed that Angie asked the customers if they would like anything else, but didn't make specific suggestions. He thought about saying something, but decided to keep quiet. Marcus checked on them at about ten, and Angie used the break in customer flow to begin refilling the cases. It appeared to have been a good morning. "How's it going?" Marcus asked, and Gregory nodded.

"Pretty well. We're out of cinnamon rolls, and the slices of carrot cake are almost gone too," Gregory told him with a smile as he wiped down the counter.

"He's a natural," Angie said as she slid a tray of cookies into the case. "He suggested something to every customer, and more often than not, they added it to their order." She moved away as a customer came into the shop. Gregory listened as she helped them. "Will there be anything else? Our doughnuts are handmade," she added at the end, and while the customer didn't take any, she looked at them and thought about it. Angie rang up their purchase, and they left the shop.

"I'll make a note to have more cinnamon rolls for next Saturday," Marcus said as he checked out the store before heading back toward the kitchen. Gregory wanted to ask him how the wedding cake was coming, but more customers came in the shop, so he and Angie got back to work.

In the afternoon, business in the shop slowed down, so Gregory spent some time with Marcus's records. They weren't in bad shape, just a little behind, so he brought them up to date and double-checked some of the entries and totals. Everything seemed in order, until he found a problem. "Is everything okay?" Marcus asked from behind him, making Gregory jump.

"I've been trying to reconcile your bakery bank accounts with your records and they don't match. They did two months ago, and then the discrepancy crept in and it was still there this month, so I'm going through those invoices to see where the error was made." Gregory had pulled out the filed invoices and receipts and was matching them to the entries. He turned, and Marcus appeared worried. "If it's what I think it is, the mistake was in your favor," Gregory told him happily. "So don't worry, I'll let you know what I find," he said before returning to the invoices.

It took him another half hour to find what was wrong, and he showed it to Marcus once he'd finished what he was doing.

"You found it?" Marcus asked as he put the finishing touches on one of the wedding cake layers.

"Yes. You entered $700 for a $200 invoice. It hadn't been written clearly, and you were probably either tired or in a hurry, so you officially have $500 more than you thought you did." Gregory liked being able to give Marcus good news. "I have everything up to date, so is there anything else you need me to do?"

"Could you help me deliver this cake? I have all the tiers done and I'm going to assemble it there rather than try to transport it whole." Marcus pulled the pastry bag away from the cake before inspecting his work. "That's that last of them." He looked over to where Becky was cleaning up. "Can you get boxes for the smaller layers, and we'll put them in the van?"

Becky made up the boxes, and Marcus carefully placed each of the tiers inside the appropriately sized box. Some were so large, they just went on big boards that held the cake safely in place. There were nearly a dozen, and Gregory followed Marcus out back and helped him load the cakes into the back of an old van.

"Teddy bought this when he and I decided to open the bakery," Marcus explained as they walked back into the store. "He paid next to nothing for it and then worked to get it running well. I only use it for deliveries because I don't want to have to replace it." They made multiple trips, and then Marcus packed a box of supplies before walking out front. "Can you handle it for a while?" Marcus asked Angie.

"Of course," she told him. "I'll send Becky home soon and then leave when you get back." Some customers came in, and she took care of them while Marcus and Gregory walked back through the kitchen.

"Thank you for everything, Becky. You did very well, and next time we'll review building and filling layer cakes," Marcus told her, and Becky beamed at him as she finished cleaning up.

"I'll help Gran when I'm done here," she said, and Marcus nodded before heading toward the back door.

"It won't take us long to get to the venue, and once I get there, I'll put the cake together and get it in their refrigerator. Then we can head back," Marcus told him as he started the engine.

True to his word, the drive didn't take too long, and they unloaded the cakes carefully, then took them into the hall. Gregory helped Marcus where he could as he put the cake together. Once everything was done, Marcus stood back, and they both admired his work. The cake was gorgeous and elegant. Marcus had purposely left room for the flowers, but other than a few spaces in the decoration for the flowers, it was glorious. Some of the staff helped them get the cake in the cooler, and they got ready to leave.

Back in the van, Marcus seemed to relax before Gregory's eyes as he got ready to head back toward the shop. "I wanted to talk to you about last night," Marcus said before starting the van.

Gregory touched Marcus's hand lightly. "I liked it." It was probably a little more forward than he was used to being, but Marcus had said nothing about it all day and he was beginning to wonder.

"Me too," Marcus said as he glanced over and then smiled. Gregory saw him lean closer, and he met Marcus halfway, their lips touching in a kiss reminiscent of the one last night, but then Gregory deepened it slightly, and Marcus took it still further, teasing at Gregory's upper lip with his tongue until he broke away. Gregory's blood seemed to be on fire, and his cock throbbed in his jeans. He was tempted to go for whatever Marcus would allow him, but guilt held him back. "It's been a long time since I've had anyone like that in my life, and the last was Teddy. I'm sort of scared," Marcus admitted.

"So am I. I've messed up my previous relationships...." Gregory swallowed, his poor history with relationships coming back to haunt him. He'd somehow managed to screw up all of them. "My track record isn't good, and most of the disasters have been my own fault," Gregory admitted.

"Sounds like we're quite a pair," Marcus said with a smile.

"I guess so," Gregory agreed, and Marcus started the engine. "But I want to try if you're willing." He couldn't let things hang like that. He had to learn to say what he felt instead of hiding it. Gregory really wanted to try. With a single kiss, Marcus had made his heart race, and Gregory felt alive in a way he hadn't in a long time, not since Sebastian.

"I'm willing," Marcus said with a smile. "I know it's kind of asking a lot, but I was wondering if you're feeling brave enough to join me for dinner tomorrow night. My stepmother is a really good cook. I'll understand if you don't want to come. Dinner with The

General can be a bit overwhelming, but I haven't taken anyone home since Teddy, and it's hard…."

"Of course I'll come. Should I bring anything? Wine, flowers for your stepmother, defensive weapons?" Gregory quipped, and Marcus chuckled.

"Just yourself is fine," Marcus said before reaching over and squeezing Gregory's hand. "I really appreciate your coming with me." Gregory turned his hand over, and Marcus slid his hand into his. Gregory looked out the window as they rode, but his entire consciousness zeroed in on where Marcus's warm, slightly rough skin touched his.

THE following afternoon, Gregory hurried through his apartment wearing only his underwear, trying to figure out what he should wear to dinner with Marcus's family. The stories Marcus had told him on the rest of their drive back to the bakery had told him The General could be formidable, and he wanted to make a good impression. He didn't seem to have any dress clothes, so he combed through his drawers until he found a pair of dark blue pants that he could wear with a white shirt. Having found what he wanted, Gregory pulled out his old ironing board, pressed the clothes so they would look crisp, and then put them on. He was just buttoning his shirt when he heard his bell.

Gregory hurried down the stairs to the front of the building, let Marcus in, and then led him back to his apartment. "It isn't much," he warned as he led Marcus into his living area.

"It's a lot like mine and it's nice," Marcus told him. Gregory was about to hurry away to finish getting dressed when Marcus touched his shoulder. Gregory turned around, and Marcus held him lightly—not that Gregory wanted to get away—and kissed him. He felt Marcus wrap his arms around him as their kiss deepened. Marcus must have just brushed his teeth because he tasted of cinnamon, but under that was all Marcus. Gregory returned the kiss, trying not to moan, but he couldn't help it, and as soon as he did, Marcus kissed him harder.

Up till now, their kisses had been light and rather tentative, but this was deeper, harder, and more sensual. When Gregory felt Marcus lighten the touch and then pull away, it was almost like part of the warmth of the room had gone with him. "Uh, I should finish getting dressed," Gregory mumbled nervously as he looked down at himself, hoping like hell that Marcus wouldn't notice the bulge in his pants. Turning away quickly, he hurried to his bedroom and found a belt, socks, and shoes and put them on before checking himself one more time in the mirror. Joining Marcus where he sat on his tiny sofa, waiting for him, Gregory asked, "Do I look okay?"

Marcus looked him up and down. "You look great," he told him with a slight crack in his voice.

"So, do you think I'll pass inspection?" Gregory asked lightly, trying to cover for the bout of nerves keeping a tight grip on his stomach.

"Definitely," Marcus said. "Because I already approve, and it doesn't much matter what The General thinks. You passed my inspection with flying colors."

"But he's your father," Gregory said. He knew what Marcus had told him, but The General was still his dad.

"I don't need his approval. I haven't in quite a while. He's my dad and I'd like him to be as proud of me as he is of the others, but I figured out a while ago that I can't force him, and I have to be myself. I started the bakery on my own, and if it's a success—"

"*When* it's a success," Gregory corrected.

"When it's a success," Marcus said with a smile, "I'll know I did it on my own without any help or influence being brought to bear by my father." Marcus sounded so determined.

Gregory was a little surprised. "Would your dad really try to influence the careers of your stepbrothers and sister?"

"He's a retired general with friends in many places. Regardless of what he says or does, they'll never know if they're getting special treatment because of their relationship with The General. I know that for what I'm doing, success or failure is because of me." Marcus kissed him again. "And maybe with some help from my friends." They both smiled. "We should probably get going." Gregory went to get the flowers he'd purchased earlier and a light jacket before leaving with Marcus.

Marcus led him to an older car and opened the door. Gregory got inside and fastened his seat belt, holding the cut flowers on his lap. Marcus started the engine and pulled away from the curb and into traffic. "Where does your father live?" Gregory asked as they stopped at the main light on the square.

"Out near the war college. Since he retired from active duty, he teaches there. It's sort of funny, because from all accounts, his students really seem to love him." Marcus accelerated when the light changed, and they continued through town, passing the bakery along the way.

"What was he like growing up?" Gregory asked.

"Controlling. He always seemed to want everything done on his time and the way he wanted it. I remember my mother and him fighting quite a bit before the divorce, and a few times she called him a Nazi. I doubt he went that far, but he can be as stubborn and tough-willed as they come." Marcus stopped at another light, and Gregory looked over at him. "He could also be incredibly fun to be around. Once, after he got home from a deployment, we were living in Maryland at the time, he rented a boat so he and I could go fishing on the Chesapeake, just the two of us. We had the best time together sailing around the bay, drowning bait. He and I spent two days out on the water, having a blast. I must have been about thirteen, and having his undivided attention was the greatest thing in the world." They continued their way through town and then out into a less built-up area.

"Did something change? Because it sounds like you have some great memories." Gregory searched his own to see if he had anything like that in his past that he'd forgotten about, and he realized he didn't. His parents had been rather normal when he was growing up, except that his dad had never been particularly demonstrative. His mother had hugged and cared for Gregory and the rest of them, but his father had always been a bit distant.

"I wish I knew," Marcus answered, pulling Gregory out of his thoughts. "As I got older, my father's expectations grew along with me, and I guess it was in high school that I really understood that I was gay and in many ways not going to be able to measure up, so I sort of stopped trying." Marcus turned off the main road and headed out toward the base of the mountain ridge at the edge of the valley.

Gregory kept quiet, expecting more, but Marcus seemed to have finished. After a minute or two, Gregory said, "I never stopped trying for my father's approval. Right up until he told me that I should do them and the world a favor and simply give up and die, I actually thought that I might someday be able to change his mind about me." Gregory knew now that would never happen. It still hurt that his father would cast him away so easily just because he didn't fit the narrow mold his father expected.

Marcus turned onto a residential street with relatively new homes and manicured lawns. All the trees were small, so Gregory knew everything had only been there a few years. Marcus continued down the road before parking on the street in front of a nice-sized, two-story home with a brick façade. There were other cars in the driveway. They got out of the car, and, holding his flowers, Gregory nervously followed Marcus up the walk.

The front door opened as they approached, and Gregory saw a thin, impeccably dressed woman in the doorframe. "I'm so glad you could come," she told Marcus, hugging him lightly. After she released Marcus, her gaze traveled to Gregory. "Is this the friend you said you were bringing? I'm Katherine, Marcus's stepmother," she said, holding out her hand.

"This is Gregory Southland," Marcus said with a smile, and Gregory handed her the flowers after lightly shaking her hand.

"It's lovely to meet you, and the flowers are beautiful, thank you. Please come on in. Most everyone's in the den—there's some sports program on, and I can't drag them away from it until the thing's over." She led them inside, talking the entire time. "There's beer and soda in the refrigerator, so just help yourself. Claude will be mixing some of his lethal concoctions in a little while." Katherine continued walking, and Gregory followed, as did Marcus, who realized they were making their way toward the cheering and laughter drifting from the back of the house. "Go on, you two," she said at the kitchen door. "Join the others. I'll be in shortly with something to eat." Marcus nodded and turned, then walked through the warmly decorated house in the direction of the shouting.

At the back of the house was a huge family room complete with a massive flat-screen television that dominated one wall, with leather sofas and chairs all positioned for their best viewing angle. Most of them were already full, and as they entered, most of the heads in the room turned toward them. "It's about time you got here," an older, silver-haired man said as he got up, checking his watch. "Katherine said you were bringing a friend."

"Dad, this is Gregory Southland. Gregory, Claude Wilson, my father." Gregory shook the older man's hand and tried not to wince at the extreme grip.

"It's a pleasure to meet you, sir," Gregory said to the stern-faced man, who seemed to eye him with suspicion. The others in the room were all looking at him.

"Gregory," Marcus's father said. "These are Marcus's brothers. Hugo is an army lieutenant." Gregory shook his hand and exchanged brief greetings. "Peter, a lieutenant junior grade in the navy, and Josh is an ensign." He pointed to each son, and Gregory shook their hands. "I try not to think less of them," Claude said, but Gregory knew he was joking. The pride he had in each of them shone like a beacon. "Our oldest daughter, Annette, just graduated from West Point and will be taking up her commission next week. Our youngest, Eileen, is still in college." He beamed at her like she could do no wrong.

"It's nice to meet all of you," Gregory said, and when Marcus motioned toward one of the sofas, he sat next to him. All eyes seemed to shift from them back to the television. They were watching baseball, which was the one sport Gregory knew a little about.

"So what do you do?" Annette asked from next to him.

"I'm a bookkeeper, and I work for a shipping company in town. I'm also helping Marcus at the bakery," Gregory answered, and she looked at Marcus with an expression Gregory couldn't quite read.

"Did you bring something with you?" she asked.

"Your brother deserves a day off, so your mother made dessert," Marcus's father said gruffly before anyone else could answer. "How's the business doing?" he asked Marcus, but as soon as Marcus tried to answer, something happened in the game and Marcus's father's attention shifted to the television. Gregory looked at Marcus with a resigned look that said this was normal. Gregory got the feeling that The General had asked the question because he thought he had to, even though he didn't give a damn about the answer.

Marcus's younger sister, Eileen, came to sit in the chair closest to them. "This is really boring," she told them. "I hate baseball—it's about as interesting as watching the grass grow."

Gregory couldn't have agreed with her more, and when she got up and left the room, Marcus followed, and Gregory went along as well. They ended up in a small, more formal living room. Obviously, this was Katherine's room, with its lacy curtains and floral-patterned furniture. "So how is the bakery doing?" she asked as they sat down.

"It's coming along. Business keeps getting better."

"Are you still working all the time?" She seemed truly interested.

"Yeah. I work a lot, but that's what it takes to get a new business started," Marcus explained. Gregory knew that Marcus worked hard, but he had to give him chops for not going into detail with his sister. Marcus had seemed more the driven than whiny kind of guy, and Gregory was pleased to see he'd been right in his conclusion.

"Where do you go to school?" Gregory asked Eileen.

"Shippensburg. I've finally decided on a major but I haven't told Dad yet. He's been pushing me to go into business, but I'm interested in psychology and human behavior, so that's what I'm going to major in. I'm also minoring in Mandarin. I'm hoping to work in national security or something like that once I graduate."

"It sounds like you have great plans," Gregory commented.

"I do," she agreed before turning to Marcus. "You really didn't bring anything with you?" Marcus grinned, and she leaped up and threw her arms around Marcus's neck. "I knew you'd bring something."

"Of course I'd never forget you and Katherine," Marcus replied, returning her hug. "There's a box in the trunk of the car with some cinnamon rolls for you to take back with you, and another box to eat here." She hurried away, presumably to Marcus's car, and Gregory sat back in the chair, looking around the room.

"I thought you might have been exaggerating," Gregory said as he reached over and took Marcus's hand. "He really doesn't want to accept you, does he?"

"I have no idea. Sometimes I think he says things like that because he might understand how hard I'm working, and other times, I think he simply can't stand that my work is something he considers for women," Marcus told him softly. "But I've decided to take him at his word for now, because the alternative hurts."

"Tell me about it," Gregory quipped, and Marcus smiled slightly.

"I think the game is just about over," Katherine said from the doorway, and Gregory tried to pull his hand from Marcus's, but he tightened his grip slightly and waited for her reaction. She stepped further into the room. "I was hoping you were more than friends," she said to Marcus, and Gregory smiled at her. "You work too hard and have been spending too much time alone." She squeezed Marcus's shoulder before leaving the room. Gregory thought they had somehow passed some small test, or at the very least received some sort of approval, which Marcus seemed to need, because his whole demeanor changed. Gregory felt Marcus's muscles relax.

"My father ignores that I'm gay, and I never expected find acceptance of any type here," Marcus whispered, "except for Eileen."

"Does everyone know?" Gregory asked, and Marcus nodded.

"I told them a while ago, but no one speaks of it," Marcus answered.

"Maybe they don't because it isn't a big deal to them," Gregory suggested. "My family railed against me. I had no doubt about what they felt because they were extremely vocal, the way most people are when they hate something or someone." Gregory tightened his grip on Marcus's hand. "There are times when I can still hear my father's voice telling me I'd be better off dead."

Marcus nodded. "Let's join the others and put this theory of yours to the test." Marcus stood, and Gregory did the same, and they rejoined the others.

The television was dark and silent as they walked into the room. A tray had been brought in with crackers, cheese, and grapes. Gregory sat down next to Marcus as some sort of argument raged about the future of US policy in Iraq. "That's enough of that," Marcus's father pronounced, and he turned to Gregory. "Our guest doesn't need to hear us argue over things we have no control over. Need I remind everyone that this is a celebration? Annette graduated from West Point at the top of her class, and we're here to celebrate her achievement and wish her well as she begins her military career." He looked so pleased that Gregory thought he was about to burst, and as he peeked at Marcus, he saw nothing but longing in his eyes. Gregory knew how he felt. Regardless of what Marcus had told him on the way over, Gregory could see that Marcus still longed for the praise and affection of his father. He wanted his father to be proud of him, and The General should be, in Gregory's opinion.

Congratulations and good wishes were shared by everyone, and Gregory shook Annette's hand, wishing her well. The conversation turned to many different topics, all going at once. He talked with Eileen for a while, as well as with Hugo and Josh.

"Say, Mom," Annette said over the din when Katherine came in and sat on the arm of her husband's chair. "You never told me what happened with the friend of yours that you were trying to help get into the Martin Derry School." Annette turned to him. "Mom had a friend whose son applied to the Martin Derry School for next year. They don't have much money, and Mom was helping them through the application process. She's volunteered at the school for years now."

Katherine looked uncomfortable, and Gregory saw her touch Claude's arm. "He didn't get in," Katherine stated, and the room quieted, everyone anticipating a story of some sort. "The school turned him down because they didn't feel like they had the facilities to ensure his safety and the safety of the other students."

"What did he have, cholera?" Hugo asked with an impish grin. The man was handsome, and Gregory thought he'd probably look impressive in his uniform. Katherine shook her head and looked at her husband, whose eyes and jaw seemed set in stone.

"What made him such a threat?" Marcus asked, and his father turned to him, the look frigid, screaming that he didn't want the subject brought up. Gregory saw Marcus look at the others, but they seemed to cower under The General's powerful expression. "For God's sake, Dad, can't you stop being The General for a few minutes and just be our father for once?" The fire Gregory saw in Marcus's eyes was impressive and damned attractive, especially when The General blinked.

"They wouldn't let him in because he has HIV. They said that they couldn't guarantee the safety of the other students at the school,"

Katherine said and looked a bit heartbroken, but Gregory felt his own anger begin to rise.

"Are they stupid?" Gregory asked before he'd had a chance to think, and he felt all eyes in the room turn to him. "HIV is spread by bodily fluids like blood, not by casual contact. There's no danger to the other students. Kids with HIV have been going to public schools with other children for decades. I thought ignorant stuff like that was a part of the past," Gregory spouted, and then he quieted when he realized everyone was staring at him.

Katherine stood, walked to where Gregory was sitting, and patted him on the hand. "Thank you," she said. "That's exactly how I felt, but the board's decision is final, and right or wrong, there isn't much we can do."

"That's just stupid," Gregory muttered as he settled back on the sofa. Marcus touched his hand lightly, and he turned and mouthed an apology to him.

"Didn't your friend Teddy have HIV?" Hugo asked, and Marcus nodded. "He was a pretty cool guy, and you lived with him for years and you never got it."

"Of course not," Marcus answered

"That's enough talk about diseases," The General pronounced as he lifted himself out of his chair. He glared at Marcus for a few seconds as if he was challenging him to say anything.

"Yes," Katherine said as she headed toward the kitchen. "Dinner will be ready in ten minutes. Eileen, could you help me get the table set?"

"We'll help," Marcus volunteered, and Gregory was happy to leave the room with him. He needed a few seconds to clear his head. Following Marcus's lead, he helped place the utensils on the table.

"I'm sorry, Marcus," he whispered as they worked. "I should have kept quiet."

"No. You said what you felt and you were right. It is stupid and discriminatory," Marcus said. Gregory looked into the kitchen as Katherine slammed one of the drawers closed and yanked the oven door open with enough force that it almost bounced closed again.

"What is it, Katherine?" Marcus asked.

"Your father hates it when I talk about Reggie, but it just makes me mad." She pulled out the roast and set it on the counter, then closed the oven door a little more gently than she'd opened it. "The board actually told them that the reason they were denying him entrance is because it's a boarding school, and they couldn't guarantee the safety of the students because they couldn't stop them from sleeping with each other."

Gregory dropped the silverware he was holding, and it clanged on the floor. He could hardly believe his ears.

"They wouldn't let Reggie into the school because he might have sex with some of the other boys," Katherine continued. "I started to wonder what in the hell kind of school are they running. I considered stopping my volunteer work, but I figured I might be able to learn something to help Reggie and his family if I stayed. Most of the teachers and faculty at the school feel that the board made a huge mistake, but they want to keep their jobs, so everyone is being very quiet." Katherine seemed truly upset as she finished getting dinner ready, and Gregory picked up the utensils he'd dropped. Marcus got clean ones, and then Gregory finished setting the table.

Katherine called everyone to dinner, and Gregory sat next to Marcus in the chair he indicated, but not before excusing himself to take his medication. The anger he'd felt earlier had turned to hurt and even a touch of shame. He liked to forget sometimes that even though decades had passed and there had been so many things learned about HIV, there was still a lot of fear and ignorance. Once everyone was at the table, Gregory tried to push those feelings to the back of his mind as everyone talked. He felt Marcus lightly touch his leg beneath the table. He knew Marcus was communicating his support and understanding with the simple gesture.

"This is excellent," Gregory told Katherine after swallowing his first bite of her roast, and the others echoed his compliment.

"So, Dad, how are your classes going this year?" Marcus asked.

The General set down his knife and fork. "Very well. I'm teaching a new class this year about the military's role in the greater American society. It centers on how service members and the military in general have contributed to society as a whole. I'm finding the class exciting and a bit of a challenge," he explained before quieting and returning to his dinner.

"Is it usual that you're all able to get together at one time?" Gregory asked.

"No," Hugo answered. "A dinner like this with the whole family is very unusual. I'll be shipping out tomorrow for a base in North Carolina, and Annette takes up her commission in the next few weeks."

"I'll be traveling to Norfolk, where I'll board my ship and be gone for at least six months, and Josh leaves for his tour early next month," Peter explained, and the others nodded slowly while Katherine dabbed her eyes with her napkin. "It's a rare treat to have all of us together in one place, and it may not happen again for quite a while," Peter added.

"Is your family in the area?" Katherine asked, after clearing her throat.

Marcus patted his leg lightly. "Gregory's family is in the area, but they don't speak," he said softly, and Gregory heard the pain in Marcus's voice, pain he was feeling for him. Gregory wanted to hug Marcus right there at the table, but instead he lowered his eyes and swallowed hard. He didn't deserve someone like Marcus. Gregory would only end up hurting him, just like he'd hurt Sebastian. Well, maybe not the same way, because Gregory knew he'd never cheat on anyone again, but he'd hurt him somehow, nonetheless. Gregory reached for his glass and took a sip, thankful that the conversation moved on and the others didn't ask for more information.

The meal continued, and Gregory nodded and smiled, taking part in the conversation where he could, but mostly he listened. They told jokes, and he laughed, even at the lame ones. After everyone had eaten, almost everyone wandered back into the family room. Gregory helped Katherine and Marcus clean up the dishes, and then Marcus began saying his good-byes. He had to be at the bakery really early in the morning.

Katherine sent them both home with a care package, and Gregory thanked her then said good-bye to everyone before following Marcus to the car. "You have a nice family," Gregory said once the car doors were closed.

Marcus sighed. "Sometimes I don't know what to think." He started the engine. After turning around in the driveway, he headed back the way they'd come earlier in the evening.

"Maybe you're reading too much into them. They seemed nice and accepting as far as I could tell. Your stepmother certainly seems to care for you."

"I know she does," Marcus agreed.

"But you wish your father would say something," Gregory prompted, and Marcus nodded.

"He always looks so proud of Hugo, Peter, Josh, and now Annette. Is it too much to ask that he'd look at me like that too?" Marcus's voice sounded as if it might break at any second.

Gregory touched Marcus's leg in the same reassuring way Marcus had touched his at dinner. "You can't *make* your father proud of you. Either he is or he isn't. But that's not your problem; it's his. If he can't see how hard you're working and can't see what a wonderful person you are, then it's his loss," Gregory told him. "I know it's hard to accept, but I had to with my family. They don't want me, and I can't change their minds for them."

"And that's their loss," Marcus whispered as he took Gregory's hand. Gregory smiled, and they rode in near silence, holding hands until Marcus pulled up in front of his building. "Would you like to come up with me?"

Gregory hesitated before saying yes. He got out of the car and followed Marcus into the building and up the stairs to an apartment a lot like his own. "Please make yourself comfortable," Marcus said, motioning to the sofa. "Would you like something to drink?"

"No, thank you," Gregory said, feeling a bit nervous. It had been quite a while since he'd been with someone he wanted to get to know, and he was damned near terrified. All his fears kept playing in his mind, and he wished there was a way for him to turn them off. Marcus sat down next to him and took his hand the way he had in the car.

"I'm glad you came with me," Marcus told him. "It was nice having you there." Marcus moved closer, and Gregory turned to face him. "You're a sweet man, Gregory," Marcus whispered as he stroked Gregory's cheek. Gregory leaned slightly into the touch and closed his eyes as Marcus moved still closer and kissed him.

Gregory whimpered softly as he tasted Marcus's sweetness. Marcus kissed like a dream, with just enough force to feel like a man, but without overwhelming him. Gregory parted his lips, and Marcus ran his tongue over Gregory's upper lip ever so lightly. He groaned softly as he was pressed back onto Marcus's sofa. All those doubts and fears that had run through his head on the way home flew from Gregory's mind as he grasped Marcus in a tight hug, holding him as the kiss continued to deepen. It had been a very long time since he'd been touched intimately, but Gregory's mind and body remembered and responded with gusto. His cock throbbed in his pants, and without thinking, he thrust against Marcus's hips and kissed him with everything he had.

By the time Marcus paused for air, Gregory was awash in a haze of passion. He wanted Marcus so badly he could think of nothing else. When Marcus climbed off the sofa, Gregory whimpered with disappointment, certain that Marcus was having second thoughts, or that he'd misread the situation somehow. Instead, Marcus took his hand and lightly tugged him to his feet and through the doorway to

Marcus's bedroom. When Gregory saw where he was being led, he nearly jumped for joy. Marcus must have seen the excitement in his expression because he smiled and guided Gregory toward the double bed. "Are you sure about this?" Gregory asked even as Marcus pressed him toward the bed. The back of his legs hit the mattress, and Gregory sat on the edge of the bed, bouncing slightly.

"Why wouldn't I be?" Marcus asked, sitting next to him and taking Gregory's hand.

"You know that sex with me is dangerous," Gregory said softly.

"I'm aware of every safe-sex practice there is," Marcus told him, stroking lightly up Gregory's arm. "If you don't want to do this, we won't. But you won't hurt me in any way, I know that." Marcus touched his cheek, and Gregory turned his head to meet his gaze. He wasn't sure he believed that. He'd managed to hurt everyone he'd cared about before.

"I'm not a good bet," Gregory said softly. "I hurt Sebastian because I was stupid and cheated on him, and I hurt my family just by being myself. I'm afraid I'll hurt you too, and this time it won't be something you can recover from." Gregory kept his voice from breaking. He wanted to be with Marcus so badly he ached for it, but he didn't want to hurt him.

"Hey. Your family isn't your fault, and as for Sebastian, he's happy and has forgiven you. So maybe it's time you did the same for yourself." Marcus tugged Gregory's collar away from his neck and began kissing him lightly. Gregory felt his entire body come alive at that simple touch. "What is it?" Marcus mumbled against his skin before continuing to kiss his way up Gregory's neck. "How long has it been since you've been with anyone?"

"Before I got sick," Gregory answered truthfully.

"So no one has touched you like this in a long time," Marcus said as he opened the buttons of Gregory's shirt, kissing down Gregory's neck and into the ever-growing V of the parting fabric.

Gregory shook his head and held his breath, hoping against hope that the wonderful sensation wouldn't end. "Sebastian and Robert hugged me when I lived with them. Sebastian was always demonstrative and caring, but that was the most that anyone has touched me in a long time, and certainly not like that," Gregory said, gasping softly when Marcus parted his shirt and ran his tongue around one of his nipples.

Marcus eased him back onto the bed, leaving his legs hanging off to the side. When Gregory felt the kisses stop, he raised his head and watched as Marcus lifted each of his legs and pulled off his shoes. Then Gregory heard Marcus's shoes hit the floor and watched as Marcus stood in front of him and pulled his polo shirt over his head. Gregory stopped himself from gasping at the sight of Marcus's flawlessly pale skin, his body stretched as he lifted his arms over his head. Marcus was beautiful; there was no doubt about that: sleek muscles, smooth skin, with a trail of dark hair that led from his belly button down into his pants. Gregory shivered slightly at the thought that he might just get to follow that trail.

Marcus climbed onto the bed, kissing him as he guided Gregory up onto the bed until his head rested on the pillows. This time when Marcus kissed him, Gregory ran his hands over the soft skin on Marcus's back. He clamped his eyes shut and let the sensation of being with Marcus fill his senses. Marcus always smelled sweet, like the scent of the bakery had gotten into his skin, and when their kiss broke, Gregory used the opportunity to see if Marcus tasted the same way. He did.

Gregory licked along Marcus's shoulder and then kissed the base of his neck. He wanted more, but Marcus moved away, and then Gregory's shirt was being tugged up and over his head. He raised his arms, and Marcus chuckled when his head got caught for a second. Then he was free of the fabric, and Marcus pressed his chest to Gregory's, warm skin to warm skin. If Gregory were honest with himself, he'd admit that he'd pretty much given up on the idea of having this kind of contact in his life again. After he'd been diagnosed, he hadn't expected to find someone who would want to be intimate with him. He knew all about safe sex and that he and his partner could be careful. It was just that Gregory hadn't expected to find someone who would want to be with him. "Marcus," Gregory groaned softly as he thrust his chest forward so Marcus could suck a little harder on his nipple.

Marcus raised his gaze to meet Gregory's. "I can almost hear you thinking. All those doubts running through your head—just let go of them and be happy. Allow yourself to feel pleasure, because you deserve it." Marcus made his point by kissing Gregory's chest as he caressed his skin. Gregory moaned softly under the caresses, and Marcus stopped for a second. Gregory nearly begged for more of Marcus's touch, but he didn't need to as Marcus caressed his cheek. Gregory leaned into his hand like a cat, moving his head into Marcus's warm, comforting touch.

Marcus settled on the bed next to him, and for a second Gregory wondered if he'd done something wrong. "Close your eyes and lie back," Marcus told him softly, and Gregory complied. Marcus's hands seemed to move everywhere—over his chest, down his stomach, and even along his shoulders and arms. He was simply being caressed, petted. "You need to be touched and held," Marcus told him in a deep, soft voice. "I think it's just been too long and you don't remember how nice it is to have someone to take care of you."

Gregory rolled his head on the pillow in agreement, keeping his eyes closed as he soaked up the gentle attention like a sponge. After a while, his head began to spin slightly, and he almost thought he was dreaming. He had to be. When Marcus opened his pants and tugged them off his legs, Gregory's entire body vibrated with excitement. Up till now, he'd been keeping his eyes closed, but as he felt Marcus caress his length through his briefs Gregory gasped in surprise, his eyes flying open. He saw that Marcus had removed his pants, as well, and stood naked by the side of the bed.

"God, Marcus, you're stunning," he half mumbled as he wriggled his hips against Marcus's hand.

"Look who's talking," Marcus retorted with a smile before slowly gripping the waistband of his briefs and then tugging them down his legs.

Marcus dropped the last of their clothing on the floor before climbing back on the bed. He covered Gregory's body with his, their cocks gliding along each other as his chest pressed to Gregory's. Legs entwined, skin pressed to skin, Marcus found Gregory's lips, and he kissed him hard as both their bodies flexed lightly, sending shock waves of pleasure through Gregory's cock to the rest of his body. "I never thought anyone would touch me like this again," Gregory said between kisses, and Marcus looked him deeply in the eyes.

"This is only the beginning, if you'll let me," Marcus told him, and Gregory swallowed and nodded before kissing Marcus with everything he had. Gregory's entire body was on fire as he thrust his hips and felt Marcus's body moving above him.

Gregory felt Marcus work his hands beneath him and he lifted his hips. Marcus's hands cupped his cheeks, and Gregory groaned loudly when he felt Marcus's fingers lightly stroke over the skin of his opening. The excitement that had been building leaped forward, and pressure from deep inside began to bubble to the surface. Gregory thrust his hips faster, closing his eyes as his release built. He heard Marcus's breathing change and knew he was close as well.

Marcus cried out, and Gregory felt him come between them, warm wetness spreading between their bodies. Gregory had opened his eyes and watched every second of Marcus's pleasure, and that sight, more than anything else, sent him over the edge as he added his own release to Marcus's.

Gregory held Marcus tight as he floated in the afterglow, relishing the firm weight of the other man on his body. He knew it was probably an illusion, but for now he felt safe and comforted, like Marcus would take care of him. Marcus kissed him lightly and then shifted onto the bed. The cool air of the room caressed Gregory, and he shivered slightly. Marcus must have felt it, because he hurried away, then returned with a warm cloth and towel that he used to clean Gregory up before joining him back on the bed.

It wasn't too late, but Gregory knew that Marcus had to get up extremely early, and he figured he'd be asked to go home at any time. Figuring it was better not to overstay his welcome, Gregory sat up on the edge of the bed and began looking around the floor for his clothes. "Where are you going?" Marcus asked from behind him.

"I figured you'd want me to get ready to go," Gregory answered, and he was pleasantly surprised when he felt Marcus lightly tug him back onto the bed. He hadn't been expecting to be invited to spend the night, but as Marcus got him settled under the covers, the lights clicked out, and Gregory felt Marcus curl up next to him, lightly stroking his chest. Gregory sighed into the darkness, immensely pleased and happy. It had been a long time since he'd felt this content about anything, let alone being with another person.

"Give me a minute," Gregory whispered before getting back out of bed. He'd almost forgotten to take his evening pills. Fishing on the floor for his pants, he pulled out the small case and headed to the bathroom. He'd figured out a while ago never to be without his next round of pills. It was just safer. After swallowing the pills with water, he left the bathroom and climbed back into bed, and Marcus pulled him close right away.

"I have to get up early," Marcus said in the darkness and then yawned. Gregory hugged Marcus tight and closed his eyes. He didn't care when Marcus had to get up. He was going to spend the night holding and being held by Marcus. That was worth any inconvenience.

It wasn't long before Marcus's light caresses ceased, and Gregory heard Marcus's breathing even out. Gregory lay still for a while, staring at the ceiling and thinking of everything that had happened that evening. For some reason, the child who'd been denied entrance to the Derry school because he was HIV positive kept running through his mind. Gregory knew exactly how Reggie felt, because he'd been discriminated against and written off by people who should have had his best interests at heart. "Go to sleep," Marcus mumbled, holding him a little tighter. "Whatever you're thinking about will wait until tomorrow."

Gregory knew Marcus was right, and he closed his eyes, letting his thoughts go.

CHAPTER FIVE

"WHAT gives?" Cindy asked as she approached Gregory's work area. His desk was covered with invoices carefully stacked into piles. Something hadn't been adding up, and his supervisor had asked if Gregory could try to find the error. He'd been narrowing in on it when Cindy approached.

"About what?" Gregory asked, placing the invoice he'd been examining on the stack of reviewed documents.

"You've been happy for the last three days, and you're still smiling even after Fred gave you the shit job that he should be doing," she explained in a whisper. "So what gives? I bet you got lucky," she added with a slight blush that probably matched the one Gregory felt bloom on his face. "You did, didn't you?" she pressed, and Gregory nodded slightly. "Well, good. You had us all worried for a while. Is he the man who made the cake you brought in?"

Gregory met her gaze. "Yes," he answered quietly.

"Lucky," she mock grumbled. "I wish I could find a man who can cook." She winked and left his desk in a hurry, meaning Fred was making one of his rounds through the office, and no one wanted to be seen talking. Gregory went back to work and found the problem invoices just as Fred approached his desk.

ANDREW GREY

"Making progress?" Fred asked from behind him. Fred was a rather old-fashioned boss. He'd worked for the company for years, and if there wasn't a rule against it, he'd probably have had a cigar clenched between his teeth all the time. Big, loud, brash, and demanding were some of the kinder words used to describe him. Pain in the ass and son of a bitch also came to mind, but Fred seemed to like Gregory, and Gregory wanted to keep it that way.

"I think I found the errors," Gregory said as he turned around, holding up the invoices causing the problem. "They appear to have been keyed wrong on our end. Thankfully, we appear to have billed the customer correctly, and they paid the right amount, so it isn't as bad as it could be."

"Who keyed them?" Fred asked right away in an almost accusing tone.

"I don't know," Gregory said, showing Fred the invoice copies. They were usually initialed by the person keying them, but these were blank. Gregory thought he knew who had keyed them, but he wasn't going to say anything. "I can fix them and make sure everything balances first thing in the morning."

Fred nodded. "Do that, and place copies of them on my desk when you're done," he said—or more accurately, commanded—and Gregory nodded before returning to his work. He had a few more to go through to be thorough, and he wanted to get that done before he left. He heard Fred walk away and got back to work.

"Thank you," Gregory heard whispered over the partition, and he tapped lightly on the wall. He could see where the mistakes made had been honest ones. He'd had trouble reading the copies and had had to verify the correct amounts with the originals. Granted, Janice should have done that when she keyed them, but he wasn't going to get her in trouble if he could help it. Fred could find out who keyed the invoices if he really tried, because the system had a tracking function, but he'd have to look, and once Gregory made the corrections, Fred would move onto something else and probably wouldn't pursue it.

Gregory finished up for the day, packing away his work before leaving the office. Susan was waiting for him in the lobby, and he followed her out to the car. He got inside and buckled his seat belt, holding his bag on his lap. "Are you working at the bakery this evening?" she asked as she started the car.

"Yes. But you can drop me at home if it's more convenient," he told her, and she scowled at him. "What?"

"I'll drop you at the blessedly nonvegan bakery," she nearly spat. "I'm already so damned tired of tofu, I could retch. And let me tell you, tofurkey does *not* taste like turkey, no matter what you do with it." Susan pulled out of the parking lot and drove into town. They didn't talk much on the short drive, and by some miracle Susan found a parking spot in front of the bakery and then followed him inside.

"Thanks, Susan," he said before heading back toward the kitchen, but she was already engrossed in the contents of the bakery case.

"I'll see you in the morning," she told him absently, and Gregory smiled. Walking to Marcus's desk, he placed his bag on the floor before joining Marcus at one of the worktables.

"Did you want to try our luck at the farmer's market? It looks like there are a lot of people there," Gregory said, and Marcus lifted his pastry bag from the cake he was working on.

"We can't get a table. All their spaces are filled for the rest of the summer," Marcus said disappointedly before returning to his work. "I really thought that could help bring in more business."

"Who says it can't?" Gregory countered. "You have trays, right?" Marcus paused in his work. "Then make some up. Put samples in cupcake cups with sample forks. We may not be able to get a table, but we can certainly give out samples and some of those wedding brochures you had made up a while ago."

"Okay, give me a minute." Marcus finished up his work and placed the finished cake in one of the refrigerators before getting out the trays. He began cutting pieces of both white and carrot cake, placing them in cups while Gregory used the computer and printer to make up a few signs.

"Can I borrow one of your clean aprons?" Gregory asked once Marcus had finished putting the last touches on the trays. When Marcus returned, Gregory put on the apron and placed some brochures in the front pocket. Then he picked up the trays and held one in each hand. "How do I look?"

Marcus grinned. "Perfectly edible, and I love the signs. 'Try A Slice of Heaven'—that's really clever."

"Wish me luck," Gregory said as he moved toward the door. He felt Marcus touch his shoulder, and Gregory slowly turned around. Marcus lightly kissed him on the lips.

"Good luck and have fun with it," Marcus told him, and Gregory smiled as he headed toward the front door. Becky was wiping up behind the counter, and she went to hold the door for him. Gregory carefully walked toward the square. There were a lot of people milling around the park area of the square. After waiting for the light to change, Gregory joined the crowd and found a spot in the shade, relatively close to a trash can.

"Try a free cake sample from A Slice of Heaven," he called, and a few people who'd been milling around walked over to him. "I have carrot and white cake," he said, and people began taking the samples from the trays. "The bakery is just down the street," he told people as they took a sample.

"Are you the chef?" a woman asked.

Gregory smiled at her. "No, I'm his assistant. He's at the bakery cooking up more wonderful desserts."

"Then I'll have to stop by, because this is amazing," she said with a smile.

"Please do, and be sure to tell Becky where you heard about us," Gregory said as he held his tray so a child and her mother could get a sample. It wasn't long before he had quite a crowd and his samples disappeared off his huge trays.

"Hello, Gregory."

Gregory stopped, nearly dropping the tray. He knew that voice, and it both thrilled and chilled him at the same time. Gregory turned around slowly, hoping it was just his imagination. "Hi, Thom." Damn, he so did not want this man showing up right now.

"Did you miss me?" Thom asked, moving closer than Gregory would have liked.

"I'm working," Gregory said. He didn't want Thom getting too close, and he backed away. There was something about Thom that he couldn't get out of his mind, though Lord knew he'd tried. Gregory had spent a lot of time trying to figure it out, and all he could come up with was that he was cursed with the worst luck on earth.

"I see that," Thom said, absently plucking a sample from the tray, and Gregory felt Thom's gaze travel up and down him. It was like everything stopped around him under Thom's smoldering gaze. Model gorgeous and as intense as an earthquake, Thom had rocked Gregory's world on more than one occasion. A slight sweat broke out on Gregory's brow, and he took a deep breath, then let it out slowly.

"What do you want?" Gregory asked with a dry mouth. "Haven't you done enough to me already?" He pulled himself out of his Thom-induced trance.

"I haven't begun with you, and you know it." Gregory felt Thom look him over again, and to his shame, his body reacted. Gregory tried to tell himself that this was only his memories being rekindled, but he wasn't sure, and the doubt shook him. "Your sweet lips say one thing, but your body quite another."

"Thom," Gregory began as firmly as he could. "It's over and it has been for quite a while," Gregory whispered so no one would hear. The last thing he wanted was for Sebastian or Marcus to see him right now. Sebastian would come unglued, and Marcus... well, Gregory didn't want to have to explain Thom to anyone. His behavior with him hadn't exactly been his finest hour.

"You know that's not true," Thom retorted in his sweet-as-honey voice. "You'll always be mine; your body knows it and you know it." Thom flashed him one of his most brilliant smiles and then slowly turned and walked away, making sure Gregory got a good view of his powerful backside. Gregory closed his eyes and turned away, offering the tray of samples to a passing woman. He had to do something to clear his mind and keep his body from shaking.

Once one tray was empty, he set it on the wall behind him and then handed out brochures along with the remaining samples. "Try A Slice of Heaven," he called when there was no one nearby, and soon he had people crowding around him again.

Gregory was almost out and about to pack it in when he saw Becky hurrying toward him with another tray. He'd been on the square less than half an hour. "Thanks," he told her as he took the tray, and she grabbed the empty ones. "This should do it," he told her, and she nodded before hurrying back in the direction of the bakery. Gregory transferred the last of his samples to the new tray and began giving them out.

"Try a cake sample! The best you've ever had!" Gregory called, and a few more people took a sample and a brochure. A very tall man approached, and Gregory grinned. "I should have known you'd be by for a sample, Your Honor," Gregory teased as Robert took a carrot cake cup. At least Robert hadn't seen Thom. Gregory regulated his breathing and pushed Thom from his mind.

"I love this," Robert mumbled as he ate the small sample.

"Then stop by the bakery. It's just down the street," he said as he indicated the direction. Gregory knew Robert was well aware of where the bakery was, but he was making a show of it for the others around, and people seemed to be responding.

"I'll stop by on my way home," Robert promised, and Gregory smiled, then went back to handing out still more samples. It wasn't long before his tray was empty and most of the pamphlets had been given out. Gathering all his things, Gregory walked back toward the bakery. If that didn't bring in some business, he wasn't sure what would, and he was right. As he approached the bakery, he walked faster as he saw people leaving and entering, the bakery doors not closing fully before they were opened again.

Inside, the store was filled with people, with both Becky and Marcus helping customers. Gregory set the trays on one of the tables, went behind the counter, and pulled on plastic gloves. "Can I help you, ma'am?" he asked the next lady in line. She explained that she wanted to place a cake order, so he grabbed the pad and helped her. Behind him, the register rang and a customer threaded his way out. Gregory completed the order he was working on, and the woman asked for a dozen cookies, as well. He placed them in a box and rang them up for her, then gave her the change and thanked her before helping the next customer. It went on like that for the next hour or so, the activity pushing Thom from his mind. For a while, every time they helped one customer, another entered, but eventually the flow slowed and they got caught up. The cases still contained some product, but Marcus explained that everything available was out in the store, and still their customers were buying.

About an hour before closing, the store quieted, with just a few customers trickling in. Becky looked like she'd been run ragged, but Marcus was radiant. "We got almost three dozen cake orders," he told Gregory as he thumbed through the sheets, "and two wedding cake appointments in addition to the ones we've gotten since that huge wedding last weekend." Gregory half expected Marcus to jump up and down, he was so excited.

"Are you going to be able to do them all?" Gregory asked, and he saw worry taint Marcus's joyous expression.

"Probably not in the long run," Marcus said with a sigh. "Maybe I can find a part-time cake decorator," Marcus added hopefully as he wandered back into the kitchen. The bell tinkled on the door, and Gregory saw a woman enter with what looked like her teenage son.

"Can I help you?" Gregory asked, and the woman approached the counter, looking a bit uncomfortable.

"Katherine Wilson asked us to stop by," she said softly. "I'm Joanna Perth, and this is my son Reggie. She said Gregory and Marcus might be able to help us." She looked confused and very unsure of herself.

It took Gregory a few seconds to make the connection from the conversation with Marcus's parents to the people standing in front of him. "Becky, can you handle the store for a few minutes?"

"Of course," she said with a smile.

"Thanks, holler if you need me," he said, and she rolled her eyes at him before grinning.

"Please come with me," he said, leading them into the kitchen, where Marcus was working on three more cakes. "Marcus," Gregory called, watching as he set down the pastry bag. "This is Joanna and Reggie; your stepmother sent them by." Marcus looked confused, but he led them to his desk and offered them each a folding chair.

Joanna sat uncomfortably, and Reggie stood quietly behind her chair. "Katherine saw me today and she asked that I speak to you. She seemed to think you might be able to help us."

"I believe this is the young man Katherine told us about Sunday before dinner," Gregory said, and Marcus nodded.

"Your son was trying to get into the Martin Derry School," Marcus said, and Joanna nodded. "And my stepmother sent you to us because she thought we could help?"

She opened her purse and pulled out a letter. "They denied him, because...." Gregory could tell how hard it was for her to talk about it. She had obviously had a tough time if it.

"It's okay," Gregory said to both of them. "We understand. I'm HIV positive as well, and I think what they did was appallingly stupid." The anger he'd felt when Katherine had first told him the story returned. "Katherine told us on Sunday what had happened, but she didn't mention that she was going to ask you to stop by."

Joanna seemed to feel a bit more comfortable, and she actually smiled. "Katherine said you would feel that way and she asked me to come by because she thought you might be able to help us. She said her stepson was a good man who would understand and do his best to help." Joanna pulled a tissue out of her purse. "She's very proud of you."

Marcus swallowed and nodded, then looked blankly at him, and Gregory thought for a few minutes before slapping his head in a "duh" moment. "I'm not sure how much Marcus and I can help you directly, but we may know someone who can," Gregory explained as ideas started running through his head.

"What are you thinking?" Marcus asked tentatively.

Gregory shrugged, because his idea was probably half-baked. "I'll try to think of something," Gregory said, looking at Marcus, who nodded. "*We'll* try," he corrected with a smile. "Give Marcus your phone number, and we'll call if we have any ideas."

"Thank you," Reggie said, speaking for the first time. Joanna stood and walked toward the front of the store, and Gregory followed them out.

"You never asked how he got it," she said to him. "That's everyone's first question."

Gregory snorted. "It doesn't matter how he contracted it. HIV is a disease, not the moral punishment some people around here would like to think it is." Gregory walked them to the front door. "I'll be happy to listen if you ever want to talk," Gregory told Reggie as they stepped out onto the sidewalk. "Dealing with this disease is a lot for anyone to process. It doesn't mean you're weak if you need to talk to someone."

"Thank you," Reggie said. Gregory wasn't sure if his offer was truly received or not. Gregory pulled the door closed behind him and then went to work, helping Becky get ready to close.

"Giving out the samples brought in a lot of business," Becky commented as she began emptying the cases, moving the items that would keep to the refrigerators.

"The trick is to see if the increase in business was long-term or short-lived," Gregory said as he cleaned up the tables inside. Once he was done, he brought in the tables and chairs from the sidewalk and locked the door. It didn't take long for the two of them to have everything closed up, and after he let Becky out, Gregory locked the front door and wandered into the kitchen, where Marcus was just taking a batch of cake layers out of the oven. "Are you about ready to leave?" Gregory asked as Marcus closed the oven door and turned it off.

"I just need to let these cool so I can put them away," Marcus said as he placed the pans on cooling racks. "Are you really going to try to help Reggie? You've never met him or his mother before tonight. What if there's more to their story than what little my stepmother told you?"

"Do you think Katherine would send someone to see you that she didn't trust and know pretty well? She said at dinner that she'd been trying to help them through the application process, so she must know them fairly well by now. Maybe we can talk to her, just to be sure. But anyone can see that they're both upset and scared." Gregory sat down on one of the stools, watching Marcus clean up. "Can you imagine being a teenager, HIV positive, and being denied access to a school because of something you can't help or do anything about because the people making those decisions are complete morons?" Gregory spat, his passion rising. "Being HIV positive is hard enough when you're an adult, let alone as a teenager." Gregory's energy seemed to overflow, and he began pacing the floor behind one of the worktables. Yes, they needed to contact Katherine, but barring some revelation, he wanted to do something. This whole situation really pissed him off.

"Do you really think you can help them?" Marcus asked.

A SLICE OF LOVE

Gregory's thoughts were going a mile a minute. "I can't alone; I know that. But I'm wondering if we don't have some friends who might be able to help," Gregory said and then realized that he was doing nothing while Marcus worked. "Do you need me to do anything?"

"No. I'm just checking on everything while these cool," Marcus explained. "It's probably going to be another fifteen or twenty minutes."

"Do you want to meet me at Café Belgie then? Or were you planning to just go home?" Gregory had hoped that Marcus would want to be with him after work, but Gregory knew he had to be understanding.

"I'll meet you there," he told him with a smile. "We can go back to my place if you like. I have something we can heat up," Marcus said as he moved closer to where Gregory was standing, "before we heat things up." Gregory tried to stop the little shiver that ran up his back, but he couldn't. "I like you this way, all full of energy and fired up. We can put that to good use later."

Gregory leered and moved closer to Marcus, pressing him back against the worktable. "I think we can find a much more interesting way for us to pass the time than me waiting for you at Café Belgie," Gregory whispered before tilting his head and locking his lips to Marcus's. He hadn't been the aggressor in their relationship so far, but this time, Gregory wrapped his arms around Marcus's neck and held him tight, kissing hard as he explored Marcus's sweet mouth. A soft moan reached his ears, and he felt Marcus's arms wrap around his waist. Gregory deepened the kiss, winding his leg between Marcus's and fitting their hips together. He felt Marcus rock slightly and Gregory joined him, his cock throbbing in his pants. "We better stop," Gregory cautioned, his breath heaving as he pulled away. His entire body thrummed with excitement, and if he wasn't careful, Gregory would end up taking Marcus on top of one of the worktables.

Marcus's eyes swirled with passion, and he heaved for breath as he stepped away. After checking the cake layers, Marcus deemed them cool enough and began removing them from the pans. He said nothing as he worked, and once all the layers had been removed, Marcus stepped to where Gregory had been watching every move he made. Marcus tugged Gregory closer by his shirt and kissed him within an inch of his life. He and Marcus dueled for control with their tongues and Gregory was about to give in when he cupped the curve of Marcus's butt and Marcus groaned loudly, thrusting back against his hands. "You like that?" Gregory asked. Marcus swallowed hard, and Gregory watched his Adam's apple bob up and down. When Marcus let his head loll back slightly, Gregory took advantage of the opening by licking a long, slow line up his throat. "I do too. I love the way your ass feels in my hands," Gregory told him, barely above a whisper. It was almost like he could feel some of the old Gregory, the one he'd suppressed and beaten down for years, coming to the surface again.

He'd been afraid of that person up till now. That was the part of him that had cheated on Sebastian and had been all about having a good time. It was also the part of his personality that had ultimately been more about getting what he wanted than being safe.

"I like this part of you," Marcus said, and Gregory felt a shiver run up Marcus's body.

Gregory stopped what he was doing and didn't move. "I don't know if I do," he admitted.

"Hey," Marcus said as he smoothed his hand along Gregory's cheek and then into his hair. "You made mistakes, and you learned from them. The fun-loving side of you is wonderful, and you don't have to hide it away. The same person who's willing to help someone he's never met before tonight is not going to hurt anyone. You're not the same person you were then, so stop beating yourself up over the past and let yourself be who you are today." Marcus rested his forehead against Gregory's in an incredibly intimate gesture. "I know what it's like to plan for the future and have it taken away. We can't live in the past. We have to live in the here and now." Marcus touched their lips together lightly. "So kiss me and make me forget everything except you for a while."

Gregory tightened his hold on Marcus's butt, his fingers gripping his butt cheeks through Marcus's pants as he kissed him possessively. More and more, Marcus was beginning to feel like his. He saw the warm looks Marcus gave him, and he let a little part of himself hope that Marcus was for real. That he meant what he said, because Gregory's heart was becoming involved and it would hurt if Marcus decided that Gregory wasn't what he wanted. Pushing those dour thoughts from his mind, Gregory instead concentrated on their kiss, heating it further until he heard a steady stream of small whimpers from Marcus and felt him carding his fingers through Gregory's hair.

When most people found out he had HIV, they were scared to touch him, so other than hugs from a few close friends, he hadn't been touched in years. When he'd explained things to his family, his father and mother had actually stepped away from him like he was garbage. But not Marcus—he kissed, touched, and held him.

They were both heaving for breath by the time they came up for air. Marcus rested his head on Gregory's shoulder, and they stood together, holding one another. "Those damned cakes better be cool enough now," Marcus whispered into Gregory's ear, "because you have me so hot, I really don't care anymore."

Gregory stepped back from Marcus so he could think clearly. "Finish up what you have to do, and then we'll leave."

Marcus nodded and moved away, taking care of the cake layers and then cleaning up the last of his mess before leading them through the bakery, turning out the lights as they went. Outside, it had started to drizzle, and they walked quickly down the sidewalk. "The one day I forget my umbrella," Gregory commented as they walked. There was little traffic at the square, and they were able to cross the street quickly, continuing on the few additional blocks to Marcus's place. Gregory's clothes were damp by the time they got inside, and he shivered slightly in the air-conditioning.

"I'll get you something to wear," Marcus said, and he hurried to his bedroom, returning a few minutes later with a pair of old, light sweatpants and a T-shirt. Gregory changed in the bathroom, then hung his damp clothes over the shower rod.

When he stepped out, he saw that Marcus had changed as well, an equally old pair of shorts hanging on his small hips. Gregory couldn't stop himself from stepping behind him, kissing his bare shoulder as he stroked Marcus's soft skin. "Do you realize we've only known each other a little over a week?" Gregory said as he kissed the base of Marcus's neck. If anyone had told him that in such a short time he'd have found a man as wonderful as Marcus, he would have told them they were full of shit.

"It seems like so much longer," Marcus said before turning around. "And I mean that in a good way." Marcus's voice had deepened, and Gregory smiled as he let his hands roam over Marcus's chest, tweaking his nipples until they pebbled under his fingers. "If you keep that up, I'll never get dinner ready," Marcus rasped, and Gregory smiled, kissing his shoulder once again, but he didn't stop his hands. He loved the way Marcus's muscles played beneath his hands. He could feel his lover's excitement building as he stroked his skin. When Marcus's legs began to shake, Gregory backed away and let him finish what he was doing. He sat on the sofa, where he could watch every move Marcus made. Gregory watched as those slender hips swayed with each step. Marcus was definitely putting on a bit of a show, which became abundantly clear when he turned around, the front of his shorts fully tented. Marcus grinned, and Gregory leered as Marcus continued making something to eat. Gregory thought about asking to help, but the kitchen was only big enough for one person, and he loved watching Marcus, anyway.

The microwave dinged, and Marcus took out a plate before placing a second one inside. He closed the door and started the oven before he brought over the hot food and silverware and placed them on the coffee table in front of Gregory. "Go ahead and eat. Mine will be ready in just a minute and I'll join you," Marcus explained as he went back to the kitchen, then returned with two glasses of ice water. The microwave dinged again, and after getting his plate, Marcus joined him on the sofa. "Please go ahead," he said, but Gregory leaned close for a kiss.

"Thank you," he said softly, and Marcus leaned into the kiss. For a few seconds, the food was completely forgotten as Gregory feasted on Marcus's lips. He'd been hard the entire time he'd been watching Marcus, but now he throbbed in the loose sweats and wanted nothing more than to tug down the shorts Marcus was wearing and swallow him whole. Instead, he gentled the kiss, knowing they would have plenty of time to be together after they'd eaten. After breaking their contact, Gregory smiled at a rumpled-looking Marcus and then began to eat. "Katherine certainly knows how to cook," Gregory commented as he ate some of the leftovers Katherine had sent back with Marcus the previous Sunday.

"That she does," Marcus agreed. "And I love it when other people cook for me. Most people are intimidated, but it's always a treat when I don't have to cook." Marcus smiled as he took a bite of the reheated roast. "It got a bit overdone, but it's still really good."

Gregory really didn't care. Overdone or underdone, he ate his dinner with an appetite he hadn't felt in years. It wasn't long before his food was gone and he'd gotten up to place his plate in the sink. When he returned, Marcus had finished, and he was stretching his hands high above his head. Gregory couldn't resist and lunged, pressing Marcus back on the sofa. Gregory took advantage of the availability of all that skin. He kissed, licked, and tasted until Marcus was whimpering and Gregory was about to go out of his mind.

"Maybe we should take this to the bed," Marcus suggested, and Gregory got off him and stood by the sofa. He tugged Marcus to his feet, and they walked to the bedroom, Gregory following right behind Marcus.

Once the door closed behind him, Gregory reached for the waistband of Marcus's shorts and tugged them down over his hips, nipping at his butt as he lowered the fabric to the floor. Marcus stepped out of them, but Gregory didn't straighten up right away. Instead he ran his hands up Marcus's legs, his hair rough on his hands. Marcus groaned deeply when Gregory ran his hands between his legs, cupping his balls lightly before skimming up Marcus's butt and back. Without saying a word, Gregory pulled off his shirt and pressed his chest to Marcus's back, savoring the rich flavors he found on Marcus's neck with his lips.

Marcus reached for his hips, pressing Gregory's sweatpants down, and Gregory moved his hips back and wriggled them as the material slipped down his legs. He didn't try to step out of them before pressing his entire body to Marcus's. "Now that's heaven," Gregory groaned as his cock slipped along Marcus's crack. He knew he couldn't go any farther without major protection, but just being skin to skin felt marvelous.

"Love this," Marcus whispered as he moved his backside back and forth. Gregory hissed softly. Marcus was one hell of a temptation, but no matter how passionate they might get and no matter how much he might want it, Gregory would never get to feel his lover's skin on him in any other way but this. He knew that and he'd accepted it a while ago, but he still regretted that he would never be skin to skin with Marcus in the most intimate way possible.

"Lie down on the bed," Gregory said, and Marcus moved away and went to lie on his back, beautiful eyes shining up at him. "Sometimes I can barely believe I'm here with you," Gregory admitted, climbing onto the bed. "I honestly thought"—Gregory paused a second—"that intimacy was closed to me forever."

Marcus sat up and hugged him, bringing Gregory with him as he reclined back on the mattress. "Nothing is ever closed unless we let it be," Marcus told him before silencing any protest Gregory might have formulated with a searing kiss.

"Wait a minute," Gregory said when they gasped for air. He looked around and saw a package of condoms on the nightstand. Opening one, Gregory rolled it down his length, to Marcus's confusion. "We forgot this last time, but we should both use condoms in the future," Gregory said before going back to their kissing.

"What do you want?" Marcus asked as their movements against one another became more frantic.

Gregory didn't have an answer. He'd always expected that he'd let his partners decide what they were comfortable with, and it took him a few seconds to formulate an answer. "Take me," Gregory gasped, and Marcus nodded, then reached over to the nightstand for the lube. Gregory took the bottle and coated his fingers, working first one and then a second into his body as Marcus watched, enraptured. He reminded himself to double-check exactly what was safe and what wasn't, but for now he wasn't taking any chances and he wouldn't allow Marcus to, either. Once he was set, Gregory lay back on the bed and waited.

Marcus positioned himself between Gregory's legs and worked his arms under Gregory's knees. Then Gregory felt Marcus's condom-covered cock press to his entrance, and his breath caught. Locking gazes with Marcus, Gregory felt him press forward, slowly opening his body before sliding inside. Gregory breathed deeply through his wide-open mouth as Marcus stretched him wide. "Jesus God!" Gregory swore. He knew Marcus was large, but the glorious stretch stole his breath, and his eyes rolled in his head as he tried not to squirm away. It had been years since he'd joined with anyone.

Marcus stopped, and Gregory panted as he tried to keep his muscles from spasming. "Relax and breathe," Marcus said soothingly, and Gregory nodded, tapping Marcus's leg in a signal for him to continue. Slowly, Marcus pressed deeper inside him. Gregory had never felt so full in his life, and he actually wondered if he could take all of Marcus. Then he felt Marcus's hips press to his butt and Gregory breathed a small sigh as neither of them moved. Marcus throbbed inside him, his cock jumping with every beat of his heart.

"Oh God, Marcus," Gregory whined when he felt him slowly begin to retreat. The drag of the huge cock over the walls of his passage damned near sent him over the edge. He swore again when it looked like Marcus was going to pull all the way out, but he stopped, with only the head of his cock inside, and then began filling him again. Gregory moaned long and low the entire fucking time. Whenever Marcus changed direction, it seemed to catch him by surprise, and soon he'd completely given up trying to anticipate what

Marcus was going to do and gave his pleasure completely over to his lover.

"You feel amazing around me," Marcus whispered after leaning over Gregory's prone body, kissing him sloppily.

"I wish…," Gregory began, and Marcus snapped his hips.

"I know, but it doesn't matter. We're here together, and that's more than enough." Marcus seemed to know what to say to make him feel better and what to do to make him forget everything but him. Marcus began moving faster, long strokes driving Gregory to the brink, and then he'd back off. Gregory wanted to come so fucking bad, but every time he reached for himself, Marcus batted his hand away.

"Do something," Gregory pleaded as he tried once again to take himself in hand. This time when Marcus batted him away, he gripped Gregory firmly, stroking long and slow. Gregory moved his hips, arching his back as Marcus stroked him faster and faster. He needed this so bad, but too damned soon, he felt the tingling at the base of his spine. It quickly spread throughout his body, and he shook on the mattress as Marcus drove deep inside him and then stilled. Just a little more was all it took, and Gregory plunged off the orgasmic cliff, free-falling for what seemed like forever as he filled the condom.

Once he could breathe again, Gregory opened his eyes to a grinning Marcus. "Are you back with me?" he asked, and Gregory nodded. "Good, because I'm not half done with you yet."

Marcus continued throbbing inside him, and Gregory removed his own condom and tied it off. Then Marcus slowly resumed his thrusting deep inside him—long, full strokes that drove Gregory out of his mind. His entire body was hypersensitive, so each sensation was heightened to the point of damned near sensory overload. He was trying to figure out how much more he could take when Gregory felt Marcus's once fluid movements become ragged. Marcus thrust deeply, and Gregory felt him throb inside his body. "That's it," Gregory crooned as Marcus stilled, and he watched the blissful look on Marcus's face as he came.

Marcus breathed slowly and deeply for a long while before Gregory felt him pull out of his body. He groaned at the separation, and once Marcus moved away, he lowered his legs to the bed, feeling totally limp and wrung out. It barely registered that Marcus was gone until he returned with a warm cloth that he used for a quick cleanup. After he dried Gregory off, Marcus went back into the bathroom, and Gregory heard the water run. He knew Marcus was cleaning up further. Sex was a messy business—that was part of the fun—but for them, the messiness could be threatening, and Gregory knew being careful also meant a careful cleanup.

The water stopped, the bathroom door opened, and then Marcus flipped off the light before joining him in the bed. "I didn't hurt you, did I?" Marcus asked as he settled next to him. Gregory closed his eyes, making a contented humming noise, and Marcus pulled him close, making small circles on his chest that got slower and slower as they both began drifting off to sleep. This was the most content and peaceful Gregory had felt in a very long time. Maybe this time it would last. Thoughts and worries of Thom threatened to push their way into Gregory's mind, but he willed them away and hugged Marcus closer.

CHAPTER SIX

MARCUS worked diligently in the bakery kitchen the following Wednesday. He'd gotten a number of cakes decorated, and, to his delight, it looked like he was finally reaching some sort of operational efficiency. He could make full cake batches rather than half or quarter batches, and the things he made for the store were likely to sell, so he found there was less waste and less that he needed to recycle into other products.

"Don't forget that after work tonight, we have a get-together at Café Belgie," Gregory said from behind him as he came in to work, and Marcus nodded without looking up. He'd known the second Gregory approached him. Over the past week, he'd become hyperaware of him. Sometimes it was his scent that announced itself, and other times it was something as simple as his footsteps. "Darryl told me he has something he and Maureen, his pastry chef, want to talk about with you."

Marcus lifted the pastry bag from the cake. "Do you know why?" he asked, both curious and intrigued.

"I saw Darryl yesterday, and he asked if I'd tell you. I'm not sure what he has in mind, but he seemed rather excited," Gregory explained before leaning in for a kiss. "I'll send Becky back. I know she's excited about being able to work with you."

Marcus nodded and watched as Gregory walked toward the front of the store. Damn, the man was adorable. He couldn't help thinking about the past week and the time they'd spent together, particularly last Saturday night and all day Sunday, when they'd gotten out of bed only to move to his sofa, which then got quite a workout. On Monday, he caught up on chores and errands as well as ordering supplies for the bakery. By Tuesday morning, Marcus had been as rested and as relaxed as he could ever remember. Even an issue with a wedding cake that had cost him an hour couldn't bother him.

"What would you like me to do today?" Becky asked as she approached.

"There are six cakes that have been filled and are ready for a skim coat. Please do that, and after I check your work, I'll show you how to properly ice a cake. Now, your first cake will be small, and once you're done, we'll decorate it together and you can take it home to your mother," Marcus told her, and Becky beamed. He had found that she and her mother were very close. From what she'd told him, not only as mother and daughter, but also as close, trusted friends.

Becky got to work, and he watched her for a few minutes before returning to his work. She had talent and was detailed and conscientious enough that she was going to do very well and would definitely become more of an asset to the bakery. Marcus finished the cake he'd been working on and added it to the pickup cooler before starting on the next one.

"Is this okay?" Becky asked.

"You're doing great. Remember that all you want is a smooth, thin coat to hold in the crumbs so that when we do the final work, it will be as perfect as possible. Now, I don't want you to hurry, but remember that you should be able to skim-coat a cake rather quickly. That will come in time, which is why I'm having you do it over and over again to train your mind and body so you can do it almost without thinking."

He went back to work, and both of them were quiet, most of the noise coming from the equipment and sounds that drifted in from the store. "Marcus," Gregory said from the doorway. "I have a customer who wishes to place a special order and I think you need to speak to her."

"Okay, I'll be right there," he answered, finishing up the task he was in the middle of. "I'll be right back," he said to Becky, and she nodded, continuing with her work. Out front, he saw a small group of ladies standing patiently together. "Can I help you?"

"Yes, I hope so. I'm Lois Chandler, the chairwoman of the Friends of the Carlisle Public Library, and we're having a fundraiser," a stately older lady explained. "We're expecting between seven hundred and nine hundred people and we need dessert. Corky attended a wedding a few weeks ago, and she said she had the best cake she'd ever eaten. She was able to find out that it was yours. As I said, this is a fundraiser, but we aren't asking or expecting you to donate the cake. We understand that you're starting out and we always try to support our local Carlisle businesses." The other ladies nodded, but Lois continued doing all the talking. "We'd like a central decorated cake that we would put on display, but most of the cake served would be plain."

"So you want to use side cakes; very practical," Marcus said. "Would you like to arrange a tasting?"

Lois shook her head. "Corky tasted your white cake at the wedding, and that's what we want."

Marcus's heart was pounding. This was a huge order that could be made relatively easily and would get him and the bakery a major amount of publicity. "Then let me get the details and I can write up your order." Other customers came into the bakery, and Gregory handled them while Marcus and the ladies talked. Marcus had to keep his mind on the task at hand in spite of wanting to keep looking at and listening to his lover.

"Very good," Lois agreed, and Marcus motioned toward one of the tables. All the ladies sat down while he got the details. Once he was done, Marcus calculated the price and presented it to her. Marcus expected her to be shocked at the amount, but she didn't bat an eyelash. Pulling out her purse, she handed Marcus her platinum card, instructing him that she wished to pay in full. Marcus rang up the payment, trying to keep his hand from shaking before presenting her with the slip to sign.

"Would you like a cup of coffee?" Marcus asked once she handed him back the slip.

"No, thank you. We have to be going, but thank you so much." Lois stood, and the other ladies did as well.

"Is that carrot cake?" one of the ladies asked, and Gregory answered her question, turning on the charm and salesmanship that had even Marcus's mouth watering once he was done describing how good the cake was.

"I'll leave you in Gregory's hands," he told them, but they were all enthralled with the contents of the cases and no longer paying attention to him.

Marcus placed the order in the book and then returned to the kitchen and got back to work, extremely pleased. He checked on Becky's work and then spent some time with her, demonstrating the techniques needed for frosting a cake. "What you're looking for is a clean, smooth, and crisp appearance at the corners, and a layer of buttercream that isn't too thick. Goopy frosting is sloppy and wasteful." Marcus used the turntable to show her how to ice a cake, going slowly and explaining each step as he went. When he was done, he gave her a measured bowl of icing and a small cake.

"Is that all I get?" she asked, and Marcus smiled.

"I can ice this cake with that much frosting and have some left over. So take your time." Marcus went back to work, icing some cakes himself. He'd purposely done it this way so she could continue to watch his technique as she worked.

They worked the rest of the evening, and Becky did very well with her cake. He gave her another one to work on, this one for the store. When she had iced it, Marcus smoothed the buttercream slightly and showed her where she needed to work on her technique before giving her another one to work on while he decorated the first one.

"You did a great job and you're going to be very good. You just need more practice and then you'll be able to frost a cake almost as well as I do. Keep it up, and in a few weeks you can learn the basics of decorating." Marcus saw Becky grin excitedly at him. "Eventually I'll show you how to bake the cake layers and mix the buttercream and cream cheese icings."

"Thanks, Marcus," Becky said, hugging him in her excitement. "I'll go see if Gregory needs help closing up." After taking off her apron, she hurried away and went into the store. Marcus finished up the last of his work and then began to break things down in the kitchen. With Becky's help, he'd gotten ahead, and he was starting to wonder if he shouldn't hire another store person and move Becky to the kitchen. He definitely needed to plan, especially if business continued to increase. By the time he finished up, the store was closed and Gregory had counted the money and prepared the deposit for first thing in the morning. For the first time Marcus could remember, he, Gregory, and Becky all left the bakery at the same time.

Becky said good night as her ride pulled up. Marcus and Gregory crossed the street to Café Belgie. "Things seem to be going well," Gregory commented as they walked.

"I know, almost too well. I keep expecting the wheels to fall off at any minute," Marcus said before reaching into his pocket. "Before I forget, Friday is payday." Marcus was thrilled that he would be able to pay Gregory his full wage rather than just cinnamon rolls. "So much has happened in the last few weeks, and I can't help thinking that most of it is because of you," Marcus said, taking Gregory's hand. He noticed that Gregory said nothing, and Marcus stopped. "What's wrong?"

Gregory shook his head. "It's all because of you. I just helped a little," Gregory said softly.

"No. You've helped more than you know. I was in a box that I couldn't get out of, and you took a chance, pitched in, and helped get things going." Marcus lifted their hands and kissed the back of Gregory's hand, and then they began walking again.

"These good things would have happened with or without me," Gregory protested lightly.

"Maybe, maybe not. But it all began to happen when you walked into my bakery and my life." Marcus smiled as they reached the restaurant. As he pulled open the door, Marcus saw a whole group of people who all turned when they walked in. "What's all this?" Marcus asked. "It looks like a war council," he added when he saw Katherine sitting with the group.

Darryl motioned them toward the last empty chairs, and he sat down, looking around the table. He knew everyone, and from the conversation, introductions had already been made.

"We're here this evening because Gregory contacted Sebastian, and he enlisted our help," Robert said as he stood, looking every bit the judge. "I believe that all of us feel very strongly that what happened to Reggie and Joanna is not right. I've passed on the contact information for the ACLU to Katherine for her to give to Reggie and his mother, and I would be very surprised if they didn't take on the case. This is exactly the type of thing that they live for," Robert stated. "Now, as for the rest of what you're planning, I shouldn't be involved. I'm an elected judge and I never know what will cross my docket." Robert stepped toward the door, and Sebastian followed him.

The restaurant door opened, and Marcus saw Joanna, Reggie's mother, step inside. "So many people," she said, and Darryl made introductions and got her a chair, placing it next to Katherine's.

"I told you they would be able to help," Katherine said, and Marcus saw her speaking softly to Joanna, presumably about the legal information that had been presented.

"How do I pay for that?" Joanna asked softly, clearly concerned.

"They will do it for free if they take the case," Sebastian explained. "Their mission is to take cases that involve the infringement of people's civil rights. I think another thing we need to do is generate some publicity. Most people don't take kindly to organizations discriminating against children, and I may have just the person to help. A few years ago, Robert and I dealt with a reporter when a group was making problems for Robert after he was elected judge. I can contact her and see if she'd be interested in doing a story. It would mean that you and Reggie would be interviewed and everyone would know who you are."

Joanna nodded slightly, but said nothing right away. "Why are all of you doing this?"

"These are good people," Gregory said. "Sebastian and Robert took me in and helped me after I got sick. Billy and Darryl helped me as well, and I think Marcus is here because his previous partner died of AIDS. In some way or another, all of us have been touched by this disease." Marcus felt Gregory take his hand under the table. "There are two parts to being HIV positive: the disease itself and the social stigma that goes along with it. We may not be able to cure the disease, but we can certainly try to mitigate the effects of the social stigma, and this is one way to do it." Gregory sounded passionate and looked radiant as he spoke. Marcus found it hot, and he squeezed Gregory's hand.

"I'll talk to this reporter. I can't see where it will hurt," she said cautiously, and Marcus could tell she was not completely convinced.

"I'll be there with you if you like," Katherine said, and Joanna clearly felt more secure. "The reporter will be looking for a story, and you have one that will tug at people's heartstrings. She won't be after you as much as she'll go after the board at the school." Katherine's gentleness surprised Marcus. He had never seen her that way, and he was really beginning to realize that he'd painted her with the same brush that he had his father. But it was plain to see she was a very different sort of person. She probably always had been, but he'd never seen it, or allowed himself to see it, maybe because he'd never had a lot of interaction with her without The General being there.

"So it looks like you have the contact for the lawyer," Gregory recapped, "and we'll get you the information for the reporter. What else do you need?"

Joanna was quiet, and Marcus saw his stepmother lean closer, whispering softly. Then Joanna said, "How long is this going to take? Reggie needs help with his schooling. He's very smart, but where we live, the schools can't help him much. That's why we applied to the Martin Derry School. It was his chance to get the education he can't get where we live."

Everyone around the table looked at each other blankly. Marcus had no answers, and obviously no one else did either. "Unfortunately, sometimes the wheels of justice grind more slowly than we'd like," Sebastian said softly.

"You've done more than I thought was possible," Joanna said as she stood. "Thank you for all your help. I need to get home, because Reggie shouldn't stay alone for too long." Katherine stood and walked her to the door, the two of them talking softly. Katherine returned once Joanna was gone.

"I can't thank you all enough," Katherine said. "I know you don't know me or Joanna very well, and I know she appreciates everything you've done. I'll help her contact the ACLU, and please send me the reporter's contact information." She paused, and Marcus could almost hear what she wasn't saying. There had to be more that could be done, but they weren't sure what it could be. To him, a fundraiser came to mind, but it wouldn't do any good until they got some publicity, and then hopefully the publicity would bring the support, financial and otherwise, that Reggie and Joanna needed.

"If we think of anything, we'll let you know," Marcus told Katherine. "We can't solve everything in one night."

"No, we can't," she agreed before hugging him tight. "I knew sending them to you was a good idea," she whispered.

"It was all Gregory," Marcus whispered back with a smile before releasing her. Katherine said good-bye to everyone and then left. Billy and Sebastian began cleaning up the coffee cups and glasses before getting the tables reset for service, and Darryl motioned for Marcus to follow him. They walked through the kitchen to Darryl's office, and Darryl motioned Marcus to a seat on the futon.

"Maureen and I both wanted to talk to you, but she asked me to speak with you tonight because she had to leave. She and I find ourselves in a bit of a situation. She does all the desserts for Café Belgie and the Acropolis, but she's finding that she wants to move to a more part-time position. It's because she wants more time with her kids. She's a talented pastry chef and can do anything with dessert you can think of, but her passion is decorating. It's what she really loves. What she was wondering was if you could use some part-time cake-decorating help. According to her, the work you're doing is up to her standards. She'd really love to work in the late mornings and early afternoons so she can be home when the kids go to and come back from school, but that doesn't fit with when I need her."

"But what about you?" Marcus asked, thrilled to death that Maureen was interested in working with him. This could be the answer to all his prayers. At heart, Marcus was a baker. The cake decorating was something he'd learned to do and did well, but he loved the baking and construction end of things more.

"That's where I believe you can help me. Your product is high enough quality that I'm thinking you could provide the desserts for the restaurants. We'd need to work through the details, but it would be more cost-effective for me to buy specialty desserts from you than to pay for a full-time pastry chef, not that I'd trust anyone but Maureen anyway," Darryl explained. "There are some special items that I'll need, like baklava for the Acropolis, and specialty mousses for Café Belgie, but if you make them for me, you can also sell them in the store. For years I've tried to do everything myself, and it hasn't been as cost-effective as I'd have liked. If you and Maureen can work things out between the two of you, this may work out well for everyone."

Marcus could hardly believe his ears. This was almost like dropping his every wish into his lap. "Has Maureen actually worked in a bakery?" He really didn't know much about her background.

"God, yes. She worked in a bakery outside Washington, DC, for a number of years. She's used to doing things her own way, but most artists are, and that's what she is."

Marcus found he was nodding like one of those bobblehead dolls. "Why don't the three of us get together in the next few days? Maureen and I can talk through details, and we can all go over a plan to transition her to the bakery and you to the product from the bakery." Marcus was so excited he could barely stand it. This was what he'd been hoping for: steady orders for product, day in and day out, to help provide a base to the business.

"Excellent," Darryl said with a huge grin. "This will help both of us *and* Maureen." Darryl stood and extended his hand. "We'll work through the details." They shook hands on their tentative deal and then rejoined the others in the restaurant dining room. Gregory sat at one of the tables talking with Billy and Sebastian, and he smiled up at him as he approached.

"Are you ready?" Marcus asked, trying to stifle a yawn, but failing. He was exhausted and just needed to go home and get to bed.

Gregory yawned as well, and they said good night to the others and left the restaurant, then walked under the streetlights toward their section of town. At his door, Marcus paused, and Gregory kissed him good night before moving away.

"Where are you going?" he asked, and Gregory turned back around.

"I figured you were tired and needed to sleep." Gregory yawned again, and that started Marcus yawning as well.

"I am too tired for our usual activities, but we could just sleep, if that's okay," Marcus offered. He wasn't sure if that was what Gregory was interested in or not. His lover's smile gave him the answer, and Gregory followed him inside and up the stairs to the apartment. They cleaned up and fell into bed with Gregory curling next to him, and, after a good-night kiss, Marcus remembered nothing more.

FRIDAY was a madhouse. Something had clicked both with him and with the town. It seemed that the word had truly gotten around, because the store was busy all day. Angie had agreed to stay the entire day, so Marcus spent the morning trying to keep up with the sales and helping in the store. The past few weeks had seen a sea change for him in so many ways. He definitely needed more store help and bakery help. Thank goodness he'd spoken with Maureen early yesterday afternoon, and she seemed as excited to be working for him as Marcus was excited to have her. She was willing to work while her children were in school, so that worked out very well. He and Angie had reviewed the state of the business, and she'd agreed that they needed to hire additional help.

"I'll be willing to put additional money into the business and work additional hours to see you succeed," Angie had said before hugging him tight. "Your mother would be so proud of you, and I think that your father will be as well once the old goat realizes the magnitude of what you're doing." Angie had squeezed him hard, and for a few seconds, he almost thought it was his mother holding him. Angie had even been able to recommend some people she thought might work out as employees in the store so Becky could eventually move to the kitchen full time. Everything was working out.

Marcus looked up as Gregory walked through the kitchen to put his things by the desk, then hurried back toward the store, but not before coming over for a quick kiss and a smile. "Was work okay?" Marcus asked.

"Yes, and Susan is out front getting something to eat before she has to go home for a dinner of nuts and twigs. She says her house is like living with the female version of Euell Gibbons right now and she needs some real food." Gregory walked away and then hurried back. "Some of her friends are having a commitment ceremony, and Susan convinced them to order their cake from us—when Kate was out of the room, that is." Gregory grinned wickedly and then hurried toward the storefront. Marcus watched him, smiling when he realized Gregory had said cake from "us." He liked the thought that Gregory felt included here.

A few minutes later, Marcus heard Gregory call him, and, looking up, he saw Katherine walking toward him. She was smiling, and he set down his pastry bag. "I know your father usually calls you, but I wanted to invite you and Gregory to dinner on Sunday. Joanna and Reggie will be there as well."

"I'll ask Gregory," Marcus answered before realizing that Katherine had probably already spoken to him.

"I know you and your dad don't get along, and I think that's a shame. Your father can be a very loving man beneath his sometimes... gruff... exterior."

"Is that your way of saying he can be a real asshole?" Marcus asked, and he saw her smile.

"I'll give you that," she began. "Your father simply doesn't understand you. He spent his entire life in the military, driven to reach the top of the top. He understands Hugh, Peter, Josh, and Annette because he's been where they are. He doesn't understand how you can get the same fulfillment from baking that he did from getting thousands of men from one continent to another, wherever they were needed, in an impossibly small amount of time because that's what was needed."

"I don't know if he ever will," Marcus admitted, not too sure how comfortable he was with this conversation. He and his father rarely spoke now except for the occasional phone call or when Katherine invited him to dinner.

"He won't if you don't let him see it. I'll tell you something about your father. He's a huge respect man, but"—Katherine looked around like she was about to share a secret—"when I first met him, I thought he was the most arrogant, self-righteous man I'd ever met, and I told him so. He was shocked, because people rarely stand up to him, and I think it was then that he decided I might be worth his time." Katherine reached across the table and patted his hand. "We'll see you Sunday." Then she left the kitchen, and Marcus got back to work, thinking about what she'd said and wondering if she was right. He didn't have time to think about it for long. He had a wedding cake to finish and then a dozen cakes to do for the store, and when Becky came in, he got her to work.

During the evening, Marcus continued working, but he was getting tired and making mistakes, so eventually he put down his tools and wandered around the kitchen, watching Becky for a few minutes and giving gentle pointers before wandering toward the store.

"Leave me alone," he heard Gregory say. "I already told you to go." He was speaking softly, and Marcus wondered if this was something Gregory didn't want him to hear. Marcus heard footsteps, and the bell rang as the front door opened. "Stay away," Gregory added.

Marcus walked into the store as Gregory closed the front door. He saw the man walking away turn to look back inside before disappearing from sight. "Is everything okay?"

Gregory started slightly. "Yes," he answered shortly before returning to the counter. Marcus watched him for a few seconds. "It was nothing I couldn't handle." Gregory smiled, and Marcus wondered if there was more to it than that.

"If you need anything, you can call me."

"I know," Gregory told him as he moved closer. Marcus returned the smile and then went back to the kitchen, still wondering if there was more to what he'd heard or if it was his imagination at the end of a long day.

By the time the night ended, Marcus was both tired and stoked. The store had had its busiest day ever, and they had sold an amazing amount of product. He'd forgotten all about Gregory's customer, or whatever that had been. With Becky's help, he'd managed to get a good start on what he'd need for the morning, so when the store closed, they all packed up and he left with the others.

"I'm so glad you aren't working as late," Gregory told him as they walked through town under umbrellas in the light rain, still managing to hold hands. "You were working too long, and I was wondering if you were going to start to make yourself sick by working so many long hours all the time."

Marcus gazed over at Gregory and smiled. He liked that Gregory cared and was worried about him. No one had really done that much since his mother. "I know I work a lot, but I really love it." Marcus had always thought that he was simply too busy to have a relationship, and he was wondering if that was where Gregory was going. Was he saying that Marcus wasn't spending enough time with him? Because he would love to spend as much time with Gregory as he could, but starting a business was hard and required extreme dedication. He hoped Gregory understood that.

"I know you do, and it's part of why I like you," Gregory said, and Marcus felt the knot in his stomach unwind. "You have passion about what you do. I sometimes wish I felt the same way about my job." Marcus paused, because Gregory had never hinted that he might not be happy in his work. "I took the job because it was what was available. I know I can do more, and I'm hoping I'll get more responsibility eventually, but right now, it's just a job and the only one I could get. I had a great junior accountant job that I loved, but when I got sick, I couldn't keep it."

"I'm sorry," Marcus said softly. He didn't know what else to say. Marcus adored what he did. In that way, he was very lucky. He'd been able to find a way to make a living that he felt passionate about. Yes, he worried every day that something would happen to undo all the progress he'd made with the business, and to see things start to come together was amazing. But he continually worried that it would all be taken away, and he knew it could.

"Are you okay?" Gregory asked, and Marcus realized he'd been standing there for a few moments without moving. "You seemed like you were someplace else."

"I didn't mean to," Marcus said, and he started walking again. "The business is coming along and starting to do well. I keep wondering and worrying if it'll all stop just as suddenly as it started, and now I'm starting to hire more people. Before it was just me, Angie, and Becky. Now there's you and soon to be Maureen, and the person I need to hire for the store. Sometimes it all gets to me. What if I hire someone and I have to let them go because business slows down? I don't really know if I can do that."

Gregory squeezed his hand a little tighter. "Hey. You don't have to feel like you have the weight of the world on your shoulders. You're an amazing baker and you care about everyone and everything at the bakery, but we're all here to help. You aren't alone." Maybe it was time for him to start believing that. Marcus nodded contemplatively but said nothing for a while as they continued their walk to his apartment.

"Did my stepmother say anything to you when she came to the store?" Marcus asked as they turned off the main street. The rain had picked up and was now coming down steadily. Both he and Gregory had picked up their pace.

"Not much," Gregory answered. "She said she was going to invite us to dinner and that Joanna and Reggie would be there. I think she has something she wants to talk about."

Marcus stepped over a puddle, then turned to look at Gregory. "How do you know? What do you think it is? She didn't mention anything to me other than coming to dinner." Marcus squinted with a touch of confusion, and he saw Gregory roll his eyes as they passed under a streetlight, like he was missing something extremely obvious. "Okay, what did she say?"

"It wasn't what she said as much as the situation. I get the feeling that your stepmother wants something. It involves Reggie and Joanna too, and I think she invited all of us to dinner for a reason. I don't know what it is, and I may be totally wrong, but that's what I think."

Marcus felt his stomach tighten again. "What do you think she could want? Maybe she's just being nice and having everyone to dinner?" he postulated hopefully. He was busy enough right now without adding anything else.

"She could be, and I think that's part of it, but I also think she has something else in mind." Gregory squeezed his hand. "It doesn't really matter because you told her we'd come to dinner, right?"

Marcus nodded. "I said I'd ask you," he explained. "I didn't know if you had plans or if you'd want to go." Marcus glanced into Gregory's eyes. "I was sort of hoping we could have the entire day to ourselves. I have running to do in the morning so I can pick up a few things at the store and stuff, but otherwise I was hoping we could spend the day together."

Gregory bumped his shoulder. "Of course, and we can even go to the store together, and afterwards we can do other things together." Gregory leered at him. "Then we can have dinner at Katherine and The General's." Gregory seemed inordinately pleased at being invited to dinner with his family. Marcus hadn't been that excited about a visit with The General in years, and yet he remembered what Katherine had told him. If she was right, then the only way to get through to The General was to actually spend time with him. Marcus sighed softly to himself. Even in his thoughts, he referred to his father as The General. There had to be something pathetic in that.

"So what do you think she wants?"

Gregory shrugged, and they continued walking. "We'll find out soon enough, I'm sure."

Marcus knew that was true. If Katherine had something she wanted, she was usually quite good about making it happen. She was rarely selfish, and she'd even gotten The General to help her on occasion. Lord help him if she recruited him in relation to this issue with Reggie and Joanna. "You're probably right. If she's planning something, we'll find out."

Marcus grew quiet as his thoughts began to wander. Katherine did want something, and if it had anything to do with Joanna and Reggie, then he could probably guess what she had in mind, or at least some of it. If he knew Katherine, she was probably already planning a fundraiser, and the thought unsettled him. Marcus tried to keep his concerns off his face. If Katherine was planning a fundraiser, then he'd do what he could, but he was so busy right now that there were limits, and she needed to know that. The thought still worried him because he didn't have much time, among other things, and saying no to Katherine was never easy. He glanced over at Gregory to see if his thoughts were somehow written on his face. Gregory simply smiled at him and squeezed his hand slightly.

"Do you want to stay at my place or yours?" Gregory asked, and Marcus swallowed hard. "Marcus?" Gregory asked quietly, his expression changing to one of concern.

"Wherever you'd like," he answered, and Gregory led them past his place and on to Marcus's.

"It doesn't matter to me, either, and you won't have to get up so early if we're at your place," Gregory explained as they continued the block or so to Marcus's building. Marcus blinked a few times to banish the selfish thoughts he'd been having.

They arrived at his door, and Marcus unlocked it before leading the way up and back to his small apartment. Gregory turned on the lights and took care of the umbrellas before going into the kitchen. Marcus hadn't thought of it much, but when Gregory was here, the apartment felt warmer and more like a home than simply a place to live. He handed Marcus a beer before getting one for himself, and then they sat on the sofa together. "So what did you have planned for dinner?" Gregory asked quietly, moving closer as he absently set his beer on the coffee table.

"I don't know, but I definitely have plans for dessert," Marcus said. He set his unopened bottle next to Gregory's before kissing him hard, his body reacting almost instantly to Gregory's touch and taste. "I want to stay here all night, but I think we better eat before we both get light-headed," Marcus said. His head was already spinning by the time they stopped kissing, and he really didn't have much interest in food, but both of them chuckled softly when Marcus's stomach made it known that *it* was definitely interested in food. Marcus got up after a final kiss and began getting some dinner together. He didn't have much, so he made ham and eggs. He and Gregory watched television while they ate. Once they were done, they curled together on the sofa, watching the rest of the show.

"Let's go to bed," Gregory whispered, and he got up and extended a hand, then led Marcus toward the bedroom. "I want you, Marcus," Gregory told him, his voice deep as he moved them toward the bed.

Marcus kissed Gregory softly, pressing him down onto the mattress. They worked together and soon they were both naked, clothes strewn on the floor. Gregory felt amazing against him as they made quiet love to each other. Gregory seemed to know exactly what he wanted and gave it to him with such gentleness and intensity. "You're wonderful," Gregory moaned as Marcus clamped his lips around a perky nipple, swirling his tongue around the areola. Gregory writhed under him, arching his back and making the most incredible sounds.

"No," Marcus whispered, flicking his tongue over Gregory's skin, his slightly salty, slightly sweet flavor bursting in his mouth. "You're the one who's amazing. You do so much for everyone you care about." Marcus moved up Gregory's body, kissing away the denial he knew was forming on Gregory's lips. "You're beautiful." Marcus kissed Gregory hard. "Warm." He licked down Gregory's neck. "Kind-hearted." He kissed across Gregory's chest.

Marcus reached to the nightstand and pulled open the drawer. He'd bought flavored condoms, and he grabbed a mint one, opened the package, and rolled it down Gregory's length. "Marcus, you shouldn't," Gregory whimpered as Marcus took Gregory's cock into his mouth. Marcus would have protested, but instead he took Gregory deeper.

Gregory groaned deeply, whimpering as Marcus bobbed his head. "Never thought anyone would do this again," Gregory admitted. Marcus hummed his response before sucking harder, trying to make sure that Gregory got as much sensation as possible through the latex. If the deep throaty sounds Gregory made were any indication, he was succeeding.

Gregory thrust upward slowly and Marcus sucked harder. Truly, he wanted to be able to actually taste Gregory, but knew this was what they had to do. Letting Gregory's cock slide from between his lips, Marcus lifted himself up to where Gregory lay open-mouthed, panting like there was no tomorrow. "You're more beautiful like this than I ever imagined."

"No, I'm not," Gregory protested, but Marcus just smiled before kissing any further argument away.

"Yes, you are," Marcus insisted. "You should see the way your eyes dance and feel the way your muscles jump under my touch. You're an incredible man, and I'm lucky to have you in my life." Marcus knew he was incredibly lucky, and the thoughts he'd had earlier flooded him with guilt.

Marcus loved the feel of Gregory on his tongue. He knew he'd like it better without the condom, but he ignored the feel of the latex and concentrated on feeling Gregory underneath. It wasn't hard to do with Gregory filling the entire room with his soft groans and mewls, and Marcus could think of nothing that sounded better, except when Gregory came, and if he wasn't mistaken, that was going to be very soon.

Gregory thrust his hips slightly, and Marcus timed the bobbing of his head to the rhythm of Gregory's thrusts. "You're going to kill me," Gregory accused between pants, and Marcus smiled slightly around Gregory's cock, sucking deeper and harder as he hummed his answer. He knew Gregory couldn't understand him, but that didn't matter. He wanted to drive his lover out of his mind, and Marcus believed that was exactly what he was doing. "I can't last much longer," Gregory said, panting, and Marcus added his hand to increase the sensation. "Don't stop, please don't stop," Gregory chanted, and Marcus kept up his pace, listening for the hitches in Gregory's breathing and the deep groan that would indicate he was right near the peak. When he heard it, Marcus paused for just a second and then sucked Gregory deep and hard. His lover plummeted over the precipice, and Marcus felt his cock throb and heard Gregory's cry as he filled the condom.

Gregory lay panting on the mattress, his eyes closed, as Marcus let his cock slip from between his lips. Marcus smiled as he knelt next to Gregory, his skin glistening with sweat, his chest rising and falling as he tried to get enough air, eyes half-lidded, mouth open, looking completely debauched and satisfied. Marcus could think of no better sight as he lay down next to him, lightly stroking Gregory's chest. "You're so beautiful right now," Marcus told him, and Gregory slowly rolled onto his side and then on top of him.

"You're the gorgeous one," Gregory countered before kissing him hard. Gregory must have remembered the condom, because he rolled off and fumbled with himself before tying it off and throwing it away. Then the bed bounced as Gregory bounded back, hugging him close as they rolled on the bed. Gregory's earlier excitement had Marcus already on edge, so it wasn't long before he thrust his hips against Gregory's smooth skin, and, with his lover's soft words of encouragement in his ears, Marcus felt his own climax approach. He hadn't meant for it to come quite so quickly, but he didn't fight it. Within seconds, he was in the throes of orgasm, panting and gasping as he felt Gregory lightly kissing and then sucking his neck. Marcus's entire body shook, and he clamped his eyes closed, arching his back as he spread liquid heat between their bodies.

Marcus seemed to float for a while and then slowly returned to earth, with Gregory stroking his back and murmuring into his ear. Without thinking, Marcus hugged Gregory tight, pressing their bodies together, and they stayed that way until Marcus realized they were in danger of becoming glued together permanently. Then he gently climbed off the bed and got a cloth and towel. After cleaning them both, he turned off the lights and climbed back into bed. Gregory curled next to him and promptly fell asleep while Marcus stared at the ceiling, lightly stroking Gregory's back, his mind racing.

He hadn't wanted to think about it earlier, but he thought he knew exactly what Katherine wanted. She was most likely trying to organize some sort of fundraiser, and the way Katherine was, she never did things by half, just like his father. The thing that bothered him was the work she was going to try to rope him into. He was so busy right now; there was no way he could take on any more. He kept telling himself that so he'd have his answer ready, even if it was only partially true. It was the thought from the back of his mind that kept trying to force itself forward, about what his customers would think, that scared the hell out of him. If Gregory knew what he was thinking, he probably wouldn't be sleeping next to him. Not now and probably never again. He hated that the idea even occurred to him, but it had taken root and wouldn't go away. Marcus knew it was rooted in the fear he had that everything that seemed to be going right at the bakery would suddenly end—he'd have to lay people off, or worse, he'd run out of money and have to go out of business, leaving himself without a job and taking part of Angie's retirement money along with it.

He could not let that happen. Marcus had decided when he opened the bakery that he would do whatever it took to make it a success. He'd worked for months, only stopping to sleep. He couldn't let anything stop him now. He'd worked too hard and too long to stop now. Marcus closed his eyes, suddenly very keyed up and unable to sleep.

"What's wrong?" Gregory mumbled as he shifted slightly, hugging him a little lighter.

"Nothing," Marcus lied. There was no use bothering him with fears that might not pan out. He hoped that was the case, that he was worrying about something that wasn't going to happen anyway. If Katherine tried to press him into helping with some sort of fundraiser, he'd do it, but as quietly and with as little publicity as possible in case his customers weren't as supportive of the cause.

"I know there's something bothering you, and if you don't want to talk about it, that's okay," Gregory said, lifting his head off the pillow.

"I'm fine, sweetheart," Marcus soothed. "I'm just thinking too much, and my mind won't turn off." Marcus shifted on the mattress and pressed his chest to Gregory's back, spooning up to him as he closed his eyes and tried to will his mind to stop churning so he could sleep. Eventually he sighed, and a rough sleep overtook him.

CHAPTER SEVEN

GREGORY knew something was bothering Marcus and had been for the past couple of days. He was quieter than usual and seemed worried and concerned. Yesterday morning, they'd gone over the books and Marcus's cash position. There was nothing unusual in that, except they usually didn't do that on Saturday morning right before the store had its busiest hours of the week. He figured it had something to do with Marcus's stepmother and the dinner they'd been invited to that evening. Gregory kept telling himself that it was just Marcus acting a little uptight about having dinner with his father and not about Thom's visit to the store. The General was pretty intense and was enough to make anyone nervous, including him. Gregory wanted The General to like him, but he also wanted Marcus to relax around him. He was his father, after all, and regardless of whether he understood Marcus being gay, he accepted him enough to still include Marcus and his boyfriend in his life. For Gregory, that seemed pretty amazing after how his own family had acted.

"Are you about ready to go?" Gregory asked as he came out of his bedroom. They'd stopped back at his apartment so Gregory could change into nicer clothes. It had been a gloriously beautiful day, and they'd spent much of it outside. That morning, Marcus had packed a lunch and they'd gone to Thornwald Park for a picnic. They'd eaten their lunch at one of the tables, played Frisbee on the lawn, and walked along paths under the trees. Gregory had seen a number of people he'd once known, friends of his parents, and most of them ignored him completely. It hurt, but he tried his best to ignore it and simply have a good time. In the late afternoon, they'd packed up their things and driven back to Marcus's, where they cleaned up, which meant sharing Marcus's small shower, and then began to get ready for dinner with Marcus's family.

"I'm all set when you are," Marcus answered as he stood from where he'd been sitting on Gregory's tiny love seat. He led the way down the stairs and locked the door behind them before continuing out to Marcus's car. They got in and rode out of town.

"There's something bothering you, I know it." Gregory reached over the console, resting his hand on top of Marcus's. "Is it dinner with your family?"

"I'm always nervous and a bit on my guard whenever I'm around my father," Marcus confessed as he turned his hand over and lightly squeezed Gregory's fingers. Gregory knew that was to try to reassure him, but he wasn't totally convinced. The last time they'd visited, Marcus had been nervous, but he hadn't been this distracted and introverted. There was definitely something worrying him, and short of confronting him and demanding an explanation, which he wasn't likely to get anyway, there was nothing he could do. So instead, Gregory kept glancing over at Marcus, wondering at the set of his jaw and the rigid way he sat in his seat.

They arrived at Marcus's parents' house, and Marcus pulled into the driveway, parking all the way forward. He didn't say anything as he got out of the car, and Gregory followed him up the walk. The front door opened as they approached, and Katherine stepped out, smiling at both of them.

"Come in, boys," she told them as they climbed the stairs, holding the door open. "Joanna and Reggie are on their way. They had a bit of car trouble, but should be here shortly." Gregory followed Marcus inside. Hearing the television tuned to some sports show, he figured The General was in back. "Go on into the family room," she said, and, as they walked toward the sound, she followed behind.

Gregory sat on the sofa next to Marcus and watched as Katherine reached to the coffee table, turning off the television. He also noticed that Marcus's father was about to protest when Katherine silenced him with a look that would instantly freeze water. Then she left the room, and The General stared at them for a few minutes. Gregory could see anger simmering below the surface, probably from being outmaneuvered.

"So how are you?" he finally asked.

"Good," Marcus answered curtly.

"Marcus got some huge orders at the bakery, and business is starting to pick up," Gregory said, ignoring the looks from both of them. He had no intention of getting caught in the middle of a staring match. "We're doing the cake for a library fundraiser, and once people taste Marcus's cake, we'll get more orders."

"It's cake," The General said rather dismissively.

"Then I guess you haven't had any of Marcus's lately," Gregory countered, looking at Marcus for a second, seeing him look uncomfortable. "Because his cake is life-changing and his cinnamon rolls will make your eyes roll back in your head. And if you haven't tried his carrot cake, you're really missing something." The General seemed a bit surprised and turned to Marcus.

"You could have brought some for your family," he charged, and Gregory watched as Marcus said nothing for a few seconds.

"And my only blood relative could stop by to see what I've done instead of sitting in sanctimonious judgment expecting to be waited on hand and foot," Marcus retorted before crossing his arms over his chest. Both men stared at each other, and Gregory wondered who was going to blink first. After a minute, it became apparent that neither was going to back down. Thankfully, the doorbell sounded, and a few seconds later, Joanna and Reggie were led into the room. Katherine made introductions and then joined them, where she jumpstarted the conversation.

"Dear," she said, turning to The General, "Reggie and his dad used to hunt. I bet he'd love to see your collection of weapons." Reggie's eyes lit up, and The General knew when he was being handled. The boy obviously was extremely interested, though, and The General smiled.

"Of course," he answered, leading Reggie out of the room. "Have you ever seen Russian weapons before?"

"No," Reggie answered excitedly, and the two of them began talking about things Gregory didn't understand until their voices faded as they headed to the basement.

Katherine seemed pleased and turned her attention to the rest of them. She left the room and then quickly returned with a tray of appetizers and drinks. "Joanna contacted the reporter and she talked to her yesterday," Katherine prompted as she handed her a cup of tea.

"It seemed very good, but I was very nervous. She and Reggie talked and talked, so that must have been good," Joanna said, looking decidedly uncomfortable. She seemed way out of her element. "He really seemed to like her."

Gregory listened but didn't say anything, and neither did Marcus, who looked ready to duck for cover at any second. Gregory figured that Katherine was leading up to something, but she wasn't ready to tell them what it was just yet. "Did you have any luck with the lawyer?" Katherine asked as she finished pouring and then passed around the plate of small sandwiches.

"I called and they seemed interested, but they asked a lot of questions that I couldn't answer or didn't understand. They said that they would have someone in our area soon and that they would contact me to talk personally." Joanna set down her cup very carefully. "Reggie is devastated. He's worked very hard for years to do the best he could in school and he deserves to go there. He'll never get the opportunities at home that he would there." She opened her scuffed and frayed bag, pulled out a wad of tissues, peeled one off, and then placed the others back inside. "It isn't fair. Reggie didn't do anything wrong, and it isn't his fault that he got this disease, but you'd think he was a bad person by the way they treated him." She dabbed her eyes. "Reggie's a good boy. He was picking up trash from behind the house when he poked his finger on something. It was a needle and…." She began to sniffle, and Gregory shifted to sit next to her.

"I understand," Gregory said. "No one here thinks any less of Reggie or you for what happened. It wasn't anyone's fault except for the careless person who just threw away their needles." God, what sort of neighborhood did they live in where drug needles got tossed behind their house? These people really did need help. He took her hand. "It's happened to me, only I'm an adult and Reggie is a fourteen-year-old boy. What can we do to help?"

"Nothing more than you already are," she answered, wiping her eyes again. "I wish the lawyers could make the school accept him. The school year will start in a few months, and if he doesn't get in soon, he'll never be able to catch up."

Gregory squeezed her hand. "Unfortunately, one of the things that goes along with this disease is stupidity and prejudice. People are afraid of it, so they make dumb decisions. I can't tell you how sorry I am that Reggie is one of the people paying that price," Gregory said softly. He wasn't sure what else to say.

"Thank you," Joanna said, barely above a whisper.

"I got the feeling you asked us here for something other than a casual meet and greet," Gregory said as he turned to Katherine. "Now might be a good time to tell us what you have cooking," Gregory prompted, feeling more vulnerable than he ever thought he would. What was happening to Reggie was hitting very close to home with Gregory.

"Yes," Katherine admitted. "I think if Reggie is going to have any sort of chance to get into the school that we need to turn up the heat as quickly as we can. I was thinking of trying to put together a benefit and see if we could possibly get the story on the news."

Gregory nodded and turned to Joanna. "What is it you want?" Gregory suddenly wondered if anyone had asked her, and from the look on Joanna's face, they hadn't. "This is your decision. I know you want Reggie admitted to the Martin Derry School, but what are you willing to pay to get it? News stories will get both of your faces plastered onto the evening news, but it will also open you up to scrutiny by your neighbors and friends. It will also open Reggie up to taunting and other issues at his school."

"You don't think it's a good idea?" Joanna asked, clearly a bit confused by all that had been thrown at her.

"I didn't say that. I meant that you need to make a careful decision about what you want and what's best for Reggie," Gregory explained, and he looked to Marcus for support and saw him nodding. "I agree that being on the news may help, but it could also hurt. I don't know. But you should think it over."

"He's right," Katherine said, and Gregory felt much better. He'd been afraid that he was insulting Katherine, and he hadn't wanted to do that at all. "I sometimes tend to get a little ahead of myself. Of course you should think it over. But I would like to get started on the planning for a benefit. If you decide you want to do this, there are going to be plenty of expenses." Katherine was a spitfire; there was no doubt about that.

Joanna nodded slowly, and Gregory looked at Marcus, who seemed to have gone pale. "What did you have in mind?"

"I don't know quite yet," Katherine explained, but Gregory could see by the look in her eyes that she had big plans. He could also see that Marcus seemed scared to death.

Gregory wondered what could have Marcus wound so tightly. Sure, a benefit would require quite a bit of work, but Katherine would be handling most of it. Gregory figured Katherine would press Marcus into doing any desserts that were required, but he didn't think that alone would be enough to have Marcus nearly shaking. There was obviously something he was missing, and Gregory reminded himself to ask Marcus about it more forcefully on the way home. He shifted his hand between them, lightly touching Marcus's hand, and he felt Marcus squeeze his fingers in return.

"I'll do the planning for the benefit," Katherine said. "But I'll need your help, Marcus." Gregory felt Marcus squeeze his fingers again and saw him swallow hard.

"Please keep in mind that the store is very busy and that I don't have a great deal of time. I'll be happy to help where I can," Marcus said, and Gregory wondered about his diplomatic answer. There was definitely something going on. Gregory knew Marcus didn't have anything against Reggie and Joanna, so it had to be something else.

"The Kalashnikov was so cool." Reggie's voice carried into the room, and then he and The General joined them. Reggie sat next to his mother and immediately reached for one of the small sandwiches. "Mom, Mr. Wilson has the coolest collection ever. He said he'd take me to the shooting range at the base and we could fire some of his guns." Reggie was practically bouncing, and Marcus's father was actually smiling. Gregory heard Marcus sigh and saw him sink back in his chair.

"Have you decided how you're going to change the world?" The General asked a little testily as he sat down. Katherine ignored him and stood.

"I need to get dinner out of the oven," she explained and left the room with Joanna right behind her.

"Were you serious about going shooting?" Reggie asked, and Marcus's father nodded.

"I'm always serious about shooting. It's a serious business. Before you leave, I'll speak to your mother and arrange a time when I can pick you up and take you to the range," he said, and Marcus sighed again. The General turned on the television and found a baseball game. Reggie was instantly enthralled, and started talking with The General like they were old friends. After a few minutes, Marcus stood and left the room without saying a word. Gregory followed him to another room at the other side of the house.

"It seems I've been replaced again," Marcus said as he plopped down on the sofa.

"Okay," Gregory said, sitting next to him. "Were you expecting anything different?"

Marcus shook his head, but Gregory knew there had been some sort of expectation set, and whatever Marcus had been hoping for hadn't materialized. "Why doesn't he even ask how I'm doing? It would be nice if he showed some interest in my life."

"Have you showed any interest in his?" Gregory asked, and Marcus looked at him with wide eyes. "You're both adults, and it seems to me the relationship with your father is a two-way street." Gregory paused for a second. "Sorry, that sounded really sanctimonious coming from a guy who hasn't talked to his father in years. I didn't mean to make it sound like things were your fault. You simply don't have much in common, I guess." They were alone in the room, so Gregory moved closer, and Marcus put his arm around him.

"Maybe it's time I face the fact that a relationship with my dad isn't going to happen," Marcus said with a sigh. They sat quietly for a while as the sounds from the kitchen and the television drifted into the room.

"Let's go join your dad and Reggie in the family room," Gregory suggested, and Marcus nodded. When they returned to the room, the game appeared to have ended, and they were watching a movie with Tom Cruise in it. It took Gregory a few seconds before he recognized it. "Is this *Valkyrie*?" Gregory asked.

"Yes," The General said.

"Cool," Gregory said, turning to Marcus. "Have you seen this?" he asked Marcus, and Marcus shook his head. "It's a fantastic movie about one of the plots to kill Hitler and end the war. There's lots of action and suspense, and it's even better because it's a true story," Gregory explained softly as he watched the movie. It was near the beginning, but just as the suspense was beginning to really mount, Katherine called them to dinner. The General stopped the DVD, and they all went to the table.

"I'd like to speak with you," The General said seriously to Marcus as they walked to the table. Gregory went ahead, leaving them alone, and waited for Marcus at the table. They came in after a few minutes, and Marcus took his seat at the table next to him. Gregory was curious about their little talk, but he kept it to himself. If Marcus and his dad were talking about anything, it was probably good.

Conversation around the table was relatively quiet. The General asked Reggie about school and what he was studying, and then they launched into a conversation about the action The General had seen. Gregory hadn't expected to find it interesting, but the stories Marcus's father told were fascinating.

"In the field, the men become like family. They have each other's backs no matter what. When I was a lieutenant, there were two men in my company. One was the biggest guy you've ever seen, Williams, and Carter was as tall and thin as they came. No matter what this guy did——work out, eat like a horse—he never gained a pound. Those two men hated each other. They spent six months goading and sniping at each other. I was afraid I'd have to have one of them transferred to maintain unit morale." The General set down his knife and fork and wiped his mouth on his napkin. Gregory had paused as well, and he noticed that Marcus had done the same thing. "We were out on patrol in an area where the Vietcong had been active, and we came under fire. We'd been ordered to sweep the area, and Williams was hit and went down. I was about to send in some of the other guys to help get him when I see Carter half carrying, half dragging Williams out of the jungle. Saved the man's life."

"What happened? Did they become friends?" Reggie asked as he continued to eat.

The General grinned. "When Williams got out of the hospital and rejoined the unit, those two started sniping at each other like nothing had happened. But yeah, they were friends. When we had a reunion a number of years ago, those two arrived and left together, still trading jibes, but now with smiles on their faces. The jibes were just their way of relating to each other. They were still brothers and had each other's backs no matter what." The General returned to his dinner, and Gregory looked over at Marcus, grinning and winking at him. He saw the same grin returned, and he noticed that Marcus was trying not to laugh.

"What's with you two?" The General asked.

"Let me guess: they came to your reunion together, left together, and neither of them had wives," Marcus said, and it took The General a few seconds to understand what Marcus was driving at. "I also bet that if you were to look them up on the Internet, you'd find they have the same address." For a few seconds Marcus's father looked like the top of his head was about to blow off. "They do, don't they?" The General nodded, and Marcus shrugged, returning to his dinner.

"Tell another story, please?" Reggie asked, and Gregory saw The General look at both of them like if he told another story, they were going to ruin that one for him too. Marcus shook his head slightly, and The General launched into another. He talked through much of dinner, but Katherine put an end to it as she was clearing the table.

"That's enough, dear," Katherine chided gently. "Save some stories for later." She patted him on the shoulder. "Go on and watch the rest of your movie. Joanna and I are going to talk for a while, and then I'll bring in dessert."

They settled back in the family room, and The General found their place in the movie. Katherine brought in cake, and they ate and watched the rest of the movie. By the time it was over, Reggie was fighting to keep awake. He and Joanna said their good-nights and left. Gregory excused himself to use the bathroom while Katherine started cleaning up.

Gregory took care of business, then washed up carefully before leaving the bathroom to return to the family room.

"Katherine's planning some big, grand to-do to help her friend," The General was saying. "And that's fine for her, she loves to do that sort of thing. But you need to be careful." Gregory continued walking closer to the room, intent on rejoining them. "I know it may not seem like it, but I know you've been working your ass off to make the bakery a success, and I'm proud of all the work you've put into it." Gregory smiled, thinking how pleased Marcus would be to hear that. "But the last thing you want is to be known as the AIDS bakery."

"That's what I've been afraid of," Marcus said, and Gregory felt as though he'd been punched in the gut. Continuing through the house, he found Katherine in the kitchen and sat quietly on one of the stools at the counter.

"They shouldn't be too much longer," she told him. "I'm just pleased the two of them are finally talking to each other. They spend almost no time together and have so little in common."

"You might be surprised," Gregory retorted snarkily without looking up from the counter. He was more than ready to go home. He'd been looking forward to spending the rest of the evening alone with Marcus, but now all he wanted was to go home to his apartment and call Sebastian so he could vent. He should have known things were too good to be true with Marcus.

Footsteps sounded on the floor, getting closer, and Gregory lifted his gaze as Marcus approached. "Are you ready to go?" Marcus asked, and Gregory got up off the stool.

"Thank you, Katherine, for everything. You're a wonderful hostess, and please let me know if there's anything I can do," Gregory said, shaking her hand and receiving a light kiss on the cheek.

"You're very welcome," she said with a smile before giving Marcus a hug. On their way out, Gregory made sure to say good-bye to Marcus's father before following Marcus out to the car. He slid into the passenger seat and closed the door, waiting for Marcus to start the engine.

Gregory spent the ride back to Marcus's staring out the side window. He wasn't interested in talking right now. He was hurt; he knew that. He'd thought he'd found a caring soul in Marcus, but now he wondered if Marcus was just feeling sorry for him and using him for extra help in the store and as a willing bed partner. He didn't want to think either of those things—they both hurt badly—but he couldn't help it.

"Why so quiet?" Marcus asked as he turned onto the main road. "Didn't you have a good time? You looked like you were enjoying yourself." Marcus sounded energetic. "I talked to my dad for the first time I can remember where we didn't end up staring at one another or with him simply issuing orders." Marcus sounded hopeful.

"Maybe you found out you had more in common than you thought," Gregory said without turning to look at Marcus.

"Not really," Marcus said cautiously. "But we talked for a while and he told me he was proud of what I'm doing at the bakery. He's never told me he was proud of anything I did," Marcus explained happily. They continued driving through town, and then Marcus parked in front of his building and got out of the car. Gregory got out with a sigh and began walking down the sidewalk toward his apartment. "Where are you going?" Marcus asked with a tap on his shoulder.

"Home," Gregory said softly without turning around. "I'll see you tomorrow. That is, if you still want me to work at the bakery." Gregory took a step away and felt Marcus's hand slip from his shoulder. "After all, you have to avoid being known as the AIDS bakery, don't you?" Gregory continued walking away as quickly as he could, looking away from anyone he met, feeling like a complete and total fool. Part of him hoped that Marcus would hurry to catch up to him and tell him he didn't mean it, but he didn't hear footsteps. As he got farther away, he walked faster and faster until he reached his apartment. Then he saw Thom coming down the steps of his building.

"I was looking for you," Thom said.

Just perfect. "What do you want?" Thom seemed to have an innate sense for times like this.

"Are you all right?" Thom asked, moving closer. Gregory thought he was going to try to hug him and backed away. Thom looked good and smelled even better. Why did he always seem to show up when Gregory was feeling vulnerable? "Whatever's wrong, I can make it all better."

For a second, Gregory actually considered it. Marcus's rejection had hurt, and Thom could definitely make him forget. He was good at that. But what about in the morning? Gregory felt his head throb as he realized what he was doing. "Like you did before? I don't think so. I've been there once and I'm not doing it again." Gregory was shaking with anger, sadness, embarrassment—and now all he wanted was to go inside. "The last time you comforted me, I ended up losing Sebastian." He wasn't going to compound one hurt with another. Been there, done that. "Just leave me alone."

"You don't want that, not really," Thom said, and Gregory stepped around him and headed toward the door. Without another word, Gregory hurried up the stairs and into his apartment, then slammed the door.

Then he let himself breathe, feeling the hurt and sadness wash over him. "I am not going to cry," he told himself even as the tears threatened to come.

He picked up the phone and called Sebastian. "What are you doing calling me?" Sebastian asked happily. "Didn't you have plans with Marcus?" Gregory could barely speak around the lump in his throat. "I'll be right over," Sebastian said, and Gregory heard the line disconnect. He closed the phone and sat on his love seat, staring blankly at the wall.

He heard a soft knock on the door. He must have locked it, so he got up and opened it. Marcus stood outside, and he nearly closed the door in his face, but instead he silently stepped back so Marcus could come inside. "If all you have to say are excuses, then you can just go," Gregory said coolly. "I've heard excuses from a lot of people all my life, and they don't mean a sack of shit."

"Those were my father's words, not mine," Marcus said.

"You agreed with them, so you might as well have said it. See, it seems you have something in common with your father after all… and mine, for that matter," Gregory said, hearing footsteps on the stairs. He watched as Sebastian stepped inside the apartment, glaring at Marcus.

"What did you do?" Sebastian accused right away, holding Gregory protectively.

"Maybe I should go," Marcus said, walking toward the door. "I didn't mean to hurt you, Gregory. I never wanted to do that."

"Then why?" Gregory asked more plaintively than he meant to. Sebastian released Gregory from his embrace and stepped back.

"I think you two need to talk. I'll be by the phone if you need me," Sebastian told him before looking at Marcus and then back at Gregory. "And I can be up here in thirty seconds." Sebastian touched Gregory's shoulder. "Listen to him. Whatever it is, just talk and listen." Sebastian left the apartment, closing the door behind him.

Gregory folded his arms across his chest, waiting for an answer.

"I'm scared, okay? And it's not of you," Marcus began. "The customers love you. Katherine has some big plans for a benefit for Reggie, and Dad and I were talking about publicity and the fact that I needed to be careful about what I let her drag me into. Katherine tends to be like Dad when she gets hold of something. She means well and she does good work, but…." Marcus faltered. "This is hard to explain, but I'll try. Let's say we have this big benefit, and somehow we get the business into the paper. A lot of people know I'm gay, I've never hidden it, but what if the bakery gets associated with AIDS in people's minds? Do you think those library ladies would buy from my bakery? They'd go someplace else, and so would the brides. I'm probably being a scared fool." Marcus sat on the love seat, holding his head. "I keep expecting the things that have been going right lately to go south and I'll be back where I started, or worse, out of business."

Gregory felt his anger and some of his hurt melt away. "It's okay to talk about these things, you know." Gregory sat next to Marcus on the love seat. "And did you ever think that maybe those library ladies might want to help Reggie and his family? You're worrying about things that haven't come to pass." Gregory rubbed

Marcus's arm lightly. "You've been working way too much and you're exhausted and probably not thinking clearly."

Marcus nodded slowly. "I guess I let my own fears run away with my reason. But if people like the board at the school can reject Reggie for being HIV positive, then what will our regular customers say?"

"If you're helping with a benefit that will help a child, then you'll probably get publicity and a lot of goodwill, so don't worry about it until Katherine comes to you with what she wants you to do. The whole benefit idea may not work out at all."

Marcus didn't say anything. He just hugged Gregory close.

"I never meant to hurt you," Marcus told him softly. "That was the last thing on my mind when I was talking to my father." Marcus swallowed and held Gregory closer. "I should...."

Gregory lifted his face away from Marcus's chest, relieved they'd talked about this. "It's okay. I think I understand now. But you don't have to do everything and worry about everything alone. You have people to help you now, so talk to us and try not to let the what-ifs affect the here and now."

Relief washed through Gregory as they sat silently in his apartment. "You really scared me," Gregory admitted, even though he didn't want to.

"I know," Marcus said softly as he smoothed Gregory's hair. "I saw you walking away and I was hurt that you didn't see things the way I did, and then I realized how what you heard must have sounded to you and I raced over here." Marcus began to shake slightly. "I got this image of you thinking you'd been rejected again, and I couldn't stand it." Marcus touched Gregory's chin, tilting his head up until their eyes met. "I don't want any of the people I love to get hurt, and I certainly don't want to be the one hurting them." Marcus kissed Gregory lightly, and it was as if all the air had been sucked from his lungs. He returned the kiss, wondering, and hoping he'd heard correctly. As the kiss progressed, he realized he'd definitely heard right. Holding Marcus tightly, Gregory gave himself over to him as the intensity of his emotions came through the deep, penetrating kiss.

By the time Marcus broke the kiss, Gregory was panting softly, his eyes wide. "Did you really just say you loved me?" Gregory asked, needing to hear the words again.

"Yes," Marcus answered with a smile. "I saw you walking away from me and the way I felt about you hit me—that I was watching the man I love walk away from me, hurting, and doing nothing about it." Marcus held him tightly once again, like he was afraid to let him go, and that was just fine with Gregory, because he didn't want Marcus to let him go anytime soon.

Eventually, they broke apart, although Gregory had no idea how long they simply sat holding each other. Time seemed to stand still for a while.

Gregory's phone rang, and he contemplated letting it go to voice mail, but it was probably Sebastian, so he picked it up and answered.

"Everything okay?"

"Yes," Gregory answered. "It's fine." He smiled at Marcus, who smiled back.

"Good," Sebastian said, sounding relieved. "Not to throw cold water, but I passed Thom as I was leaving the building."

"I know, he's back," Gregory said, moving into the kitchen to get something to drink, lowering his voice. "I told him to stay away."

"He's lucky I didn't deck him on sight."

"What happened wasn't all his fault, you know. But if you did, maybe he'd get the message."

"As long as you aren't falling for his crap," Sebastian said.

"I'm not. I've got something much better." Gregory smiled at Marcus again. "See you later." Gregory hung up and tossed the phone on the table before moving back into Marcus's embrace.

Once they separated, Gregory led Marcus toward his bedroom. "I know us talking doesn't totally alleviate your fears," Gregory said as he pressed Marcus back onto the bed. "I don't want to be a threat to you or your business, because I love you too, and want you to be successful and happy."

"It's you that makes me happy," Marcus whispered. "My work days are really long, but I look forward to seeing you each and every day you work. Before I met you, I buried myself in my work and told myself it was what I needed and wanted to do. Now I look forward to when you come into work." Marcus grinned as they settled on the bed. It didn't matter that they were both still clothed; the way Marcus held him and touched him was as intimate and special as being skin to skin... almost. It wasn't long before their kisses increased in intensity, their touches becoming more frantic and demanding. Gregory's shirt and pants seemed to work themselves off his body as he worked open the buttons of Marcus's shirt and pants with his own dexterous fingers.

He'd been wrong—there was nothing that compared to being skin to skin with Marcus, nothing in the world. Gregory clung to Marcus, holding him tight as their movements and kisses intensified. When Marcus entered him, it was like their worlds came together. Marcus loved him, and it showed in each touch, every gesture, and the way he nearly drove Gregory crazy before pushing them both over the peak of passion. Gregory felt as though he completely came apart as his release washed over him, and when he returned to himself, Marcus was holding him tight. "I love you, Gregory," Marcus whispered over and over. Four little words that Gregory hoped to hear again and again for the rest of his life.

CHAPTER EIGHT

MARCUS placed the cake he'd been working on in the cooler and then closed the door with a smile. The past two weeks had been some of the best he could remember. Maureen had started working at the bakery, and she was amazing. Her cakes turned out gorgeous every time, and to his surprise and delight, she understood the way things needed to be done for efficiency and cost control. She'd had some ideas and practices that she'd used at the restaurant that would work very well at the bakery, so they'd adopted those as well. Becky continued to improve, and she and Maureen got along well. They rarely worked the same hours, but a few times Maureen had adjusted her hours so she could specifically work with Becky, and they were becoming good friends as well as colleagues.

"Are you still planning to hire someone for the store?" Becky asked as she finished the cake she was working on, showing it to Marcus.

"Looks good," Marcus told her with a smile. "And yes, I am. Angie and I want to give it a few more weeks to make sure everything is really going to work out, and then we'll hire someone for the store, and you can work in the kitchen more or less full time." She seemed extremely pleased as she placed the cake in the cooler for store pickup and then returned to work. At this point, she was doing mostly standard cakes for store sales. He and Maureen were handling special orders and wedding cakes, but Maureen had taken hours of work off his plate. Thank God, because he had three wedding cakes to get done for this weekend.

"Angie," Marcus said, looking up as she came through the door to the kitchen. "What are you doing here this late?" Marcus continued working as she strode over to him.

"Hi, Grandma," Becky said with a smile as she began work on another cake, this one a chocolate cake that Maureen had given them the recipe for. And while Marcus had been initially resistant, he had to admit, her recipe was richer and yielded a better cake that the customers seemed to adore.

"Hi, sweetheart," Angie said without her usual energy.

"Is something wrong?" Marcus asked after putting down his tools and following Angie to the back of the kitchen. Angie turned around and looked toward Becky, who was looking back at both of them. Angie was obviously conflicted and appeared a bit stricken.

"I have to go into the hospital next week, and I don't know exactly how long I'll be or when I can return to work. The doctors said it could be up to six weeks before I'll be able to return to work full time."

"Is it serious? Are you going to be all right?" Marcus asked quickly, and Angie patted his shoulder.

"I'm going to be fine. I have to have a bit of women's things taken care of," Angie explained. "I tried to put it off, but the old quack is adamant that I have it done right away. We'll have to figure out how we can cover what I've been doing," Angie said softly, obviously not wanting Becky to overhear.

"Don't worry about that. Just concentrate on getting well," Marcus said, because he knew it was the right thing to say.

Angie narrowed her eyes and hardened her jaw. "Don't give me that. We have to find someone, because I don't want you going back to working day and night. I know you will, but I also know you've been a whole lot happier these last few weeks, and that's because of

Gregory and the fact that you're actually spending some time away from this place." Angie knew him so well. "I want the bakery to succeed, but not at the cost of you running yourself into the ground."

"Okay," Marcus told her, trying to put the best light on this that he could. But he had to agree. Even with the help he had now, there was more work than he could do if Angie was gone, because he couldn't be in two places at once. "We'll figure something out," Marcus said, trying to reassure both her and himself.

"I know, but I hate to leave you like this," Angie said, and Marcus nodded. He knew Angie cared about the bakery almost as much as he did.

"It'll be all right. You need to take care of yourself," Marcus told her, hugging her tightly. He was closer to her than he was to his own family. "I'm going to miss you so much while you're gone." He felt her return the hug.

"I love you too," she said softly, and then she turned and walked to where Becky was working. He couldn't hear what she said to her, but Becky nodded, looking concerned, and then went back to work.

"I'll see you after work," Angie told Becky, and then she left the kitchen without her usual springy walk. Marcus wanted to collapse into his desk chair. Everything had been going so well. He tried telling himself it was only temporary, but the weeks Angie would be gone were going to be busy, if the order book was any indication. Then there was the wedding show that he'd already sent the application in for. Trying his best not to worry about it, he went back to work because it was the only thing he could do. He had to think how and where he was going to get some store help he could trust for a few weeks.

He'd just gotten back into his groove when Gregory called to him from the doorway to the store. Looking up, he saw his stepmother standing there too. He waved her over, and Gregory smiled at him briefly before returning to work. "What are you doing here?" he asked once he'd been hugged and kissed. He motioned to one of the stools, and she pulled it closer. "I have to get this done," he explained as he went back to work.

Thankfully, Katherine got right to the point. "I know you don't watch much television, but Joanna and Reggie were interviewed on two of the local television stations, and they're getting a lot of support. People have been calling the stations asking what they can do to help." She sounded so excited. "Reggie was adorable in the interviews and came across as a kid wondering why people would hate him. It was pretty powerful."

"That's great. I'm glad people want to help." Marcus spun the cake and smoothed the icing with a flat-edge scraper.

"So, to capitalize on this interest and help keep their cause in the spotlight, we're planning a benefit for them. The ACLU has agreed to help them legally, but there are other bills, including Reggie's medical costs, that are nearly crippling for them." Katherine slid off the stool. "The school's board of directors is acting like a bunch of asses, and instead of giving in like I thought they would, they're hoping this whole thing will blow over."

"Do they know you're involved?" Marcus asked, looking up from his work, and Katherine shook her head. "You know you'll have to stop volunteering soon or you could hurt Reggie's case if it comes to court."

Katherine shrugged. "I haven't done anything wrong or improper. They don't pay me, so they don't have any real say over what I do, but yes, I'm going to stop in the next week or so." She began pacing the floor behind him. "The thing is, I was wondering if I could count on your help with the benefit." Marcus was about to open his mouth when Katherine continued. "All I need help with is the desserts." Katherine leaned over his worktable, swiping her finger through a bit of icing that had dribbled. "I know what your father told you and I could just kill him for it," she said after pulling her finger out of her mouth. "I gave the old goat an earful, and he's lucky I didn't hit him. We're getting a lot of support from across the community. Even the ladies' circle from church is helping. AIDS bakery!" Marcus could tell she was still fuming about that remark, and Marcus still felt pretty bad about how he'd reacted to it as well. To think he'd hurt Gregory over that remark, and how he'd felt at the time.

"How many people are you expecting?" Marcus asked.

"We're hoping for a thousand," Katherine answered, and Marcus swallowed hard and took a deep breath, his mouth hanging open.

"I can't donate that much product," Marcus said, dang near dropping his pastry bag. "We're talking hours of work and almost $500 in ingredients to make that much cake."

Katherine looked disappointed. "I was hoping we could do desserts other than cake."

Marcus shook his head and tried to clear his mind. "I know this is a benefit, so we need to think."

"I've got some businesses that are willing to donate items," Katherine suggested. "What if I could get people to donate the ingredients? In that case, it would be mostly your time, and we could probably get people to help if you needed it."

"When is the benefit planned?" Marcus asked, his legs nearly shaking. He didn't want to disappoint her.

"A little over a month," Katherine said, and Marcus groaned out loud. "We need to do this before interest and sympathy wanes, and that can happen pretty fast."

"When it rains, it pours." Marcus looked to where Becky was cleaning up her work area. "I'm going to be short Angie for four to six weeks." He took a deep breath and thought for a while. He could bake the cakes ahead of time, and maybe Maureen would be willing to donate some time. Gregory probably would too. "We can probably come up with something, but you'll have to give me some time to think about it. Do you have the exact date? And if you say June 26, I'm going to die. That's the bridal show we're doing." *Why does everything have to happen at the same time?*

"We haven't set the date yet, though it will be during the week because the hotel that's donating the space has specified that, but I'm looking at mid-June, something like the sixteenth."

"Thank God for small favors," Marcus said as he got up and walked toward the front of the store. Gregory took one look at him and stopped his cleaning.

"What's wrong?"

"Nothing, everything." Marcus sighed loudly, thankful they were between customers. "I'll tell you everything once we close." He grabbed the order pad and walked back to where Katherine waited. He wrote down what she wanted, and they agreed on cake, but an assortment of flavors, including his special carrot cake.

"Do something flashy as a centerpiece, even if most of the cake will be normal," Katherine explained. "That'll get people's attention, and you'll get some business from it." Marcus made notations about all the details. "I'll let you know the exact date by Monday."

Marcus agreed and put together a quick list of the more expensive ingredients, including the butter, sugar, carrots, cream cheese, and eggs. Katherine's eyes boggled when she saw the amounts Marcus specified. "All this?"

Marcus nodded and smiled. "You wanted dessert for a thousand people—it takes a lot of cake to feed that many." Marcus took a bit of delight in watching Katherine's eyes widen. Becky had asked to leave early, and she said good-bye on her way out, leaving just him and Katherine in the kitchen.

"So what's wrong with Angie?" Katherine asked once Becky was gone.

"She has to have surgery, and I get the feeling Becky doesn't know yet. Angie's talking to her tonight," Marcus explained.

"You're worried about her," Katherine stated, and Marcus nodded.

"I'm going to really miss her. She's a good friend and it's going to be hard with her gone, and that was before the dessert for this benefit. I'm still trying to figure out how I'm going to get everything done," Marcus said as he went back to work, trying to finish up the cake he was working on. "I'm not ignoring you. I just need to get this done or I won't be able to go home tonight."

"I should be going anyway." Katherine leaned over the table and kissed his cheek. "Thank you for helping. It really means a lot." She stepped away, and Marcus heard her footsteps on the floor. "You know we're here if you need help."

"Thank you," Marcus said, and he smiled at her before returning to the cake he was working on.

Marcus worked steadily until it was time to close. Somehow he got everything done and cleaned up by the time Gregory closed the store and brought the money back to put in the safe. "So what's going on?"

Marcus explained what Katherine had told him and gave Gregory the condensed version of what was happening with Angie. "I don't know what else could happen to make the next few months more difficult. I signed the bakery up for the bridal show, but with Angie gone, the benefit, and God knows what else, I don't see how we can do it. Everything seems to be happening all at once." Marcus closed the safe door and made sure it was locked before standing back up. Gregory simply looked back at him rather blankly. "What happened?" He'd been running on about his own concerns, and he hadn't seen Gregory's lost expression until now.

"My mother came into the store this evening," Gregory said.

"What did she say?" Marcus asked. "Did you talk?"

Gregory shook his head. "She didn't recognize me until I turned and we were sort of face to face. I heard her gasp, and she placed her hand over her mouth and stared at me for a few minutes before turning and leaving the store." Gregory looked stricken, and Marcus forgot his own concerns and hugged Gregory tight. "She didn't even talk to me. My own mother didn't even say anything to me when I was standing in front of her."

Marcus's heart ached for him. He couldn't imagine the excruciating hurt of being snubbed by your own mother. Gregory buried his face in Marcus's chest, and Marcus slowly rubbed the back of his lover's head, wanting more than anything to be able to take the pain away. "I'm so sorry," he said softly. At least when his mother had passed away, Marcus knew that she'd loved him, no matter what. Yes, he missed her and had his bakery because of her, but he knew that no matter where she was, she still loved him and watched over him. Clamping his eyes closed, he felt his own grief, dulled slightly by time, force its way to the surface. It had been a while since he'd felt her loss this acutely, but Gregory's pain had brought his own into clear focus again. "She didn't say anything at all?" Marcus asked, and Gregory shook his head.

"She gasped and then left the store with a shocked look on her face," Gregory answered as he wiped his eyes. "I should have expected something like this eventually. They wrote me off years ago, and I don't know why I allow it to hurt anymore."

"But it does," Marcus stated, "because you still hope they'll come around. That's only natural."

Gregory nodded but didn't say anything more about it, resting his head on Marcus's shoulder for a while. "Can we go now?" Gregory asked, and Marcus nodded. "Good," Gregory added, but he made no effort to move away. "I can't understand why this hurts so much." Gregory hugged him like he was never going to let him go, which was just fine with Marcus.

Marcus understood exactly why it hurt, for the same reason he tended to stay away from his father. It hurt less when the source of the pain—or in his case, disappointment—wasn't staring you in the face. "Let's go home," Marcus said softly, and Gregory moved away. After turning out the lights, they left the bakery and walked down the quiet streets. The late spring air still held a crispness that would soon be gone, replaced by summer's sultry nights. "I love this time of year," Marcus commented to break the silence that had descended between them. "The nights are still cool enough to sleep, but the days are warm and sunny." He wound his arm around Gregory's waist, pulling him a little closer, and he heard Gregory sigh. He knew he was still thinking about his mother, probably still seeing her surprised expression in his mind. "I wish there was something I could do to help."

"There isn't anything anyone can do," Gregory said as they continued walking. "I have to accept that they don't want anything to do with me, and there's nothing I can do to change it."

"Well, it's their loss, not yours," Marcus stated a little more vehemently than he intended, but at least he saw Gregory smile slightly. "If they don't want to see you, then they're the ones missing out. They will never know what a caring, loving person you are, or how you'll do what you can to help anyone in need." As if to prove Marcus's point, Gregory stopped at one of the benches on the square and talked quietly to a man sitting there, watching people pass. After a minute, he waved and rejoined Marcus as they continued on their way. "See what I mean?" Marcus said as he took Gregory's hand.

"That's Sweeper. He used to be homeless, but Billy and Sebastian helped him get back onto his feet. He's really nice, if a bit quiet," Gregory explained as they walked away from the square, closer to home.

"Why do I get the feeling there's a story there?" Marcus asked, and Gregory smiled for the first time in a while.

"There is, but you'll have to ask Sebastian," Gregory told him before lapsing back into silence, and Marcus figured Gregory was once again thinking about his mother. Staying quiet himself, he held Gregory's hand until they arrived at his apartment. After he unlocked the door, Marcus led them upstairs. In the living room, Marcus was about to heat something for dinner when his phone rang. It was Katherine's and his dad's number, and he answered it right away.

"Marcus, what were you thinking?" His dad's forceful voice came through the phone.

Marcus sighed. "What is it, General?" Marcus asked with all the patience he had left after the day he'd had.

"I thought we agreed about this whole benefit thing," his father said, and Marcus shook his head. He shouldn't have been surprised that his father let Katherine think he was shifting to her point of view. Make a strategic retreat if needed and then come back with all guns blazing. "Now, I understand you've agreed to help Katherine and even do most of the work for free. I understand being charitable, but can you afford to do that right now?" For a second, Marcus thought his father might actually be thinking about him in some twisted sort of way. But Marcus figured The General was upset because he hadn't followed his advice.

"Sometimes doing something because it's the right thing to do is more important than what other people might think," Marcus told his dad. "I'm an adult and perfectly capable of making my own decisions. After all, I started my own business and have worked to hopefully begin to make it successful without your help." Marcus took a deep breath to try to keep his temper under control as he glanced over at Gregory, feeling much better as his lover moved closer. "You're pretty free with your opinion all of a sudden, so I'm going to give you a bit of advice. If you want your second marriage to fare better than your first, then maybe you should support your wife and what she's doing instead of trying to torpedo things behind her back." Marcus thought he heard The General actually sputter slightly, and he cursed softly. The last thing he wanted was to make him angry, and he'd deliberately antagonized him. "Sorry, that was uncalled for."

"You bet it was, young man," The General retorted.

"Well, anyway, it was nice talking to you. I'll be sure not to tell Katherine about this little conversation and consider it a bit of a mistake on both our parts to have had it in the first place." His dad said nothing, and Marcus figured this was another of those strategic retreat moments for The General. He could almost hear the man planning his next bit of strategy. "Good night, Dad." Marcus sighed and hung up the phone, then tossed it with more force than necessary onto the sofa.

"The General?" Gregory asked, and Marcus nodded. "I take it I don't want to know."

"You're correct. You don't," Marcus said, not wanting to upset Gregory with something neither of them could change. The General was who he was, and Marcus wasn't going to apologize or allow him to hurt Gregory. That had happened once with his help; it wasn't going to happen again. "He's being himself, and I'm not going to let him drag me into that again." Flashes of the hurt look he'd put on Gregory's face a few weeks earlier went through his mind, and he reached for Gregory, pulling him into a deep hug. "I'm not going there." Gregory returned the hug, and the two of them stood in the silent room for quite a while.

Marcus made something quick to eat, and then they both cleaned up and fell into bed. It had been an exhausting and emotional day for both of them, and neither made a move beyond holding each other and kissing. "I'm sorry," Gregory said after a while.

"What for?" Marcus asked as he tightened his arms around Gregory's chest. "Love is more than simply passion and not being able to keep our hands off each other. It's being there for one another and helping each other when we're troubled or hurting." Gregory angled his head upward, and Marcus kissed him softly. "It's about tender moments like this when it's just us, and there's no place I'd rather be." Gregory shifted until he was on top of him. "And there's no place I'd rather be than right here with you." Marcus gently pulled Gregory to him, their kisses starting warm and soft, but quickly deepening as Gregory poured more and more into them. Marcus felt the energy behind Gregory's kisses becoming more frantic.

Gregory was actually shaking as Marcus rolled them on the bed, pressing his lover against the mattress. He kissed Gregory deeply, peering into his eyes and seeing the reassurance he needed there.

Marcus kissed his way down Gregory's neck, paying special attention to that spot that made him writhe and moan, before licking and sucking Gregory's nipples until Gregory's legs shook with anticipatory excitement. Reaching for the nightstand, Marcus found the condoms and rolled one down Gregory's cock and then his own. Gregory moaned softly when Marcus stroked his length, and without letting him take a second to think, Marcus sucked him deep and hard, listening as Gregory gasped in passionate surprise. Marcus understood Gregory's need to have everything he was feeling taken away, and he proceeded to do his best to do just that.

Gregory thrust his hips lightly, groaning deeply as Marcus sucked him to damned near oblivion. When he felt Gregory getting close, Marcus pulled away and then heard Gregory's whine turn into a moan as he rolled on a finger cot and slipped his finger into Gregory's body. Up till now, his lover had done his own preparations, but Marcus didn't want him to do that any longer, so he'd brought home what he called finger condoms, and the effect was exactly what he'd been hoping for. When Marcus curled his finger slightly, Gregory jumped and cried out softly as he found that spot deep inside his lover. "You're so hot like this," Marcus said as he rubbed the small spot. Gregory arched his back, and Marcus saw his eyes roll back in his head.

Carefully, Marcus withdrew his finger and settled between Gregory's legs. He positioned Gregory's ankles on his shoulders and slowly pressed into his lover's unbelievably tight heat. Marcus loved the way Gregory's body opened to him and the soft mewls Gregory made as he slowly sank deeper into him. Marcus paused a few times before seating himself deep in his lover's body, his hips pressed to Gregory's butt. Marcus leaned over his Gregory, kissing him deeply, their bodies joined. "I love you so much, sweetheart," Marcus said between kisses, and Gregory tugged him down, kissing him hard, thrusting his tongue into Marcus's mouth as he took complete possession of the kiss.

"I love you too," Gregory whispered as a tear ran down his cheek. Gregory wiped it away and made little movements with his hips. Slowly, Marcus began to thrust, being careful not to hurt his lover, but Gregory had other ideas and moved hard and fast against him. Marcus let Gregory set the pace, thrusting hard, deep, and fast, accompanied by his lover's pants and moans that turned into almost a steady stream of encouraging dirty talk. Up till now, Gregory had never done that before, but he seemed really into it now. "Yes, fuck me like you mean it."

Marcus gave Gregory whatever he asked for, and soon they were both covered in sweat as they moved together. "I will," he responded, snapping his hips and growling softly as he quickened his pace. Gregory seemed to love every second of it, his voice getting loud enough at times that Marcus worried about the neighbors, but Gregory was so hot, and felt so damned good, he went with it, and it wasn't long before Gregory began making the deep resonant sounds that told Marcus just how close his lover was. Marcus wrapped his hand around Gregory's cock, stroking as fast and hard as he could, as his lover gasped, thrusting into Marcus's fist.

"So close," Gregory gasped, and Marcus tightened his grip, feeling Gregory throb as he came, clenching his muscles. The sudden tightness and the sight of Gregory in ecstasy pulled Marcus into his own splendidly mind-swirling release.

Marcus tried not to collapse onto Gregory, but he had no energy left at all. Somehow he managed to slowly pull out of Gregory's body, both of them wincing at the loss of connection, before settling on the bed next to him. They both took care of their condoms, and then Gregory curled next to him, holding Marcus tight, and it wasn't long before they both dropped off to sleep.

MARCUS woke and checked the clock before listening in the quiet room. It was two o'clock, and something wasn't right. It took him a second to realize that the bed was soaked and Gregory was bathed in sweat. Pushing off the covers, he stroked Gregory's forehead and found his lover burning with fever. "Sweetheart, wake up for me," Marcus said, and Gregory groaned. Marcus reached over to the nightstand and turned on one of the lights. "Open your eyes," he pleaded and breathed a small sigh of relief as Gregory's eyelids fluttered open.

"Don't feel good," he whispered.

"I know. You have a high fever. Can you get up?" Marcus asked, and Gregory slowly sat up, holding his head in his hands and groaning loudly.

"Everything hurts," he mumbled, and Marcus began looking around for fresh clothes. He found Gregory a pair of light sweatpants and a T-shirt, then helped him get them on before pulling on his own clothes. Then he put on a pair of shoes before helping Gregory to his feet and into a pair of his old slippers. "Where are we going?"

"To the hospital," Marcus answered. With Gregory's fever this high, there was no way he was taking any chances. Gregory might only have the flu or something similar, but Marcus knew from his experiences with Teddy that it didn't pay to risk it. Not with Gregory's compromised immune system. Slowly, he guided Gregory out of the bedroom and through the apartment, grabbing his keys and cell phone along the way. They had to be careful on the stairs, but eventually they got to street level and into the car. Marcus swore he hadn't taken a single breath until he was sitting in the driver's seat. Gregory seemed so weak he had barely been able to propel himself the last few steps. Marcus started the car and took off, taking the ten-minute drive to the hospital as fast as he felt was safe.

He pulled the car under the portico of the Emergency entrance and flagged someone down. The orderly brought a wheelchair, and then he and Marcus helped Gregory into the chair. They were rushed through the entrance and back to a private room, where an admitting clerk asked Marcus for Gregory's information, and then he almost instantly found himself shooed out into a small room. He was instructed to put on an isolation gown and gloves, then he was brought back to Gregory. A nurse and a doctor came in shortly afterward, and Marcus explained what had happened and the symptoms Gregory seemed to have.

"There's a strain of influenza that's been going around, and it looks like that's what he has, but we need to be sure," the doctor stated, and Marcus nodded. "With his immune system, we can't be too careful."

"He doesn't have his medication with him," Marcus explained, and the doctor nodded before asking a myriad of questions that Marcus didn't know the answers to. Who was Gregory's doctor? What did he take and how often? What was Gregory's medical history? Marcus knew almost nothing, and the doctor ended up getting the information from Gregory through a slow, rather halting process. Thankfully Gregory could talk and was pretty coherent, because if the doctor had been relying on what Marcus knew, they would have been in trouble. That thought scared him. They hadn't been together that long and hadn't discussed things like that yet. Marcus wondered what else he should know about Gregory, but didn't. The answer that hit him was "probably quite a bit."

"We're going to call his doctor and get specific details on his medications. We're also going to start an IV to rehydrate him and give him something to help him fight the infection. I'm also going to order a few tests to make sure it isn't something worse than what we think."

"Thank you," Gregory rasped, and the doctor squeezed Gregory's hand before leaving the room. "You don't have to stay," Gregory told him once the doctor had left. "You have the bakery to take care of."

"Shhh," Marcus soothed as he took Gregory's hand. There was no decision to make. If it was between Gregory and the bakery, then the bakery could remain closed for the day. "I'm not going to leave you alone, so close your eyes and try to rest." Marcus watched as Gregory closed his eyes, and after a few minutes, it appeared that he was indeed asleep. That lasted until the doctor came back in with the nurse. They suited up and ushered Marcus out of the room. When he was allowed back inside, Gregory looked even more tired than before and had an IV in his arm. Marcus took his other hand and did his best to try to soothe Gregory back to sleep. It didn't take long before he drifted off.

Marcus sat in the chair next to the bed and pulled out his phone, thankful he'd remembered to grab it with his keys. "Sebastian, it's Marcus. Gregory's sick and I took him to the hospital. Please call me," he said into voice mail and then hung up. He didn't know who else to call, and a few moments later his phone vibrated.

"Is he all right?" Sebastian asked frantically, and Marcus could hear him moving around.

"They think it's the flu but want to be sure. I'm at the hospital with him. They've started an IV and he's sleeping now." Marcus spoke as quietly as he could.

"I'll be right there. I don't have to be in to work until noon, so I can sit with him while you get the bakery open," Sebastian said as Marcus heard what sounded like a door closing in the background. "I'll be dressed and out the door in ten minutes." The line went quiet and Marcus stared at the dark phone. After placing it back in his pocket, he sat back in the chair and once again held Gregory's hand.

The next thing he knew, the door opened and Sebastian and Robert came in, both wearing gowns. "They insisted until they know more," Sebastian explained with a dramatic roll of his eyes. "How is he doing?" Sebastian whispered, and Marcus stood so one of them could have the chair.

"He's been sleeping, which is good, and he doesn't feel nearly as warm. They think it's the flu," Marcus explained, and Gregory stirred. "They're going to be moving him to a room soon, I hope." Marcus received a hug from both of them. "You both didn't need to come," Marcus said.

"It's all right," Robert answered, stepping to the edge of the bed. "He's a good friend." Robert looked at Gregory for a while and then turned to Marcus. "And so are you. Now go on and take care of things at the bakery. One of us will be here to sit with him, and we'll call you when they move him."

Marcus hated to leave, and he leaned over the bed, lightly kissing Gregory on the cheek. Gregory stirred, opening his eyes. "Are you leaving?"

"I have to open the bakery, but Sebastian and Robert are going to stay with you, and I'll be back as soon as I can." He leaned close, his lips near Gregory's ear. "I love you and I'll see you very soon." He saw Gregory smile, and his heart damned near broke at the thought of leaving him.

"Go," Gregory told him. "I'll see you after work." He held out his hand. Marcus held it for a minute before letting go and leaving the room before he changed his mind. He hurried out to the car, climbed in, and drove to the bakery. After parking the car, he sat inside for the longest time staring up at his storefront. When he finally got out of the car, he locked it and then got his store key out, his hand shaking as he tried to get it into the lock.

"You okay?" Angie asked from behind him, and he jumped, nearly dropping his ring of keys before he managed to open the door and step inside.

"What are you doing here?" She usually didn't work Saturdays.

"Since I'm going to be out soon, I figured I could lend an extra hand now," she explained as she turned on the lights. "What happened to you? Were you up all night?"

"Gregory's sick, and I drove him to the hospital," he answered, walking into the kitchen, where he turned on the lights and got the oven heating. "Sebastian and Robert are sitting with him." He hated that he couldn't be there. "You'll have to run the store, because I'm going to need Becky as much as I can today." He could barely think straight, and as he pulled the bread out of the proof box, he nearly dropped it on the floor.

"I don't know if I can," Angie admitted, and the more Marcus thought about it, the more he knew she was right. Gregory could handle the customers better than anyone else in the bakery. He never seemed to be in a hurry, and yet even when they were busy, he could get the customers handled and out the door faster than anyone else without making a single one feel slighted or pushed. "We're going to need some help," Angie added.

Marcus agreed, but the only person he could think of who might be able to help was Maureen, and she had the kids today. "Then we'll put Becky out front, and I'll handle things back here," he told Angie, wondering how he was ever going to be able to keep up with all the work to be done. What the hell was he going to do when Angie was gone? He was really starting to think he was going to have to live at the bakery for weeks in order to keep up with everything. As it was, he'd be lucky to get out of the bakery before eight o'clock tonight, and more than anything he wanted to be with Gregory.

Angie began mixing up the batter for the doughnuts, something he usually did, but she simply smiled at him. "What? You think I haven't watched you do this a million times?" she said, following the formula from one of Marcus's recipe cards. "You do the other things that need to get done. I'll take care of this."

Marcus got the bread in the oven and reviewed the book for what he had to get done today. He'd really been counting on having Becky in the kitchen, and without her, it looked like he would have to work late into the night, which was the last thing he wanted. Marcus didn't want to be at the bakery—he wanted to be with Gregory in the hospital, and he was so conflicted he could hardly think. He knew he needed help. They could make it through today, but with Angie out and Gregory not able to help, they were definitely going to be shorthanded. Marcus began dividing up all the work to be done, figuring out what he could put off until tomorrow when the store was closed, and what he had to get done today. Once that was done, he realized the work was manageable, and he got to it, thinking of Gregory the entire time and wondering what the hell he would have done if this had happened while Angie was out. His heart raced at the thought, and he had to take a few seconds to get himself focused before returning to his work.

THE last customer had left the store. Angie and Becky had been run ragged, and Marcus was exhausted from the pace of his work and from a near total lack of sleep. He'd spoken with Sebastian earlier in the day and learned Gregory had been moved to a room and at the time was resting. His fever was down, which was good, but the results of the tests the doctor had run weren't back yet. Gregory himself had called a few hours ago, sounding much better. He'd been alone, and Marcus felt guilty as hell that he couldn't be there with him.

"Don't stay at the hospital too late," Angie scolded as she and Becky got ready to leave. "I know you'll work yourself to the bone, but get some rest. You won't help yourself or Gregory if you get sick too."

"I promise," Marcus said with a smile, crossing his hand over his heart. "I'm going up to see Gregory for a while and then going home to bed."

"Are you working tomorrow?" Becky asked. "I can come in to help you if you need it."

Marcus yawned and shook his head. "I got almost everything done I needed to, and I called Maureen to bring her up to speed. She's agreed to come in early to help me finish." Marcus yawned again. "I think we all need a day off after the one we had today." Marcus hugged both of them. They'd been real troupers, with Angie sending Becky back to help him whenever things got slow in the store. They said good night, and Marcus locked the door behind them. After he took care of the register and the final closing, he left the bakery and headed home. At his apartment, he showered quickly and heated some dinner in the microwave before rushing out the door to the hospital.

He arrived at Gregory's room and pushed the door open. Gregory appeared to be asleep, but as soon as Marcus stepped inside, he opened his eyes and smiled. "I was waiting for you," Gregory said as he shifted slightly. "I take it you had a busy day?"

"I did. Angie came in, and the customers ran both her and Becky ragged for most of the day. Thank God we're closed tomorrow," Marcus said as he moved to the side of Gregory's bed, taking his hand. "How are you?"

"Better," Gregory answered. "They took the IV out, and the doctor said all my tests looked good. He believes I have the flu.

Things like that can come on really fast. The last time he was in, he said that getting me here as quickly as you did saved me from much worse." Gregory squeezed Marcus's hand. "He expects that I should be able to go home tomorrow or Monday."

"That's great," Marcus said as he sat down in the chair, yawning once again. "Sorry. It was really busy today, and it's only going to get busier with Angie out."

"The doctor said it would be at least until the latter part of next week before I can return to work," Gregory explained, and Marcus sighed. There was nothing he could do. Gregory's health was more important than anything else. They could manage for a few days, but even Gregory coming back didn't alleviate the long-term problem.

"I just want you to get better. Today was the longest day I can remember, because I kept thinking about you," Marcus said, bringing Gregory's hand to his lips. "I nearly burned the bread and wrote your name on every cake I decorated. Angie probably would have slapped me if she wasn't so worried and nervous about her surgery."

"You know, I think I know someone who might be able to help you in the store while she's gone," Gregory told him, eyes alert and his voice steady with maybe a touch of excitement. "I've had plenty of time to think." He held out his hand, and Marcus stared at it. "Give me your phone," Gregory said, and Marcus dug it out of his pocket and handed it to Gregory. Marcus wondered exactly what he was doing. He pressed the numbers and waited. "Katherine," Gregory said before coughing. "Yes, I'm going to be fine. I got the flu and ended up in the hospital because it knocked me for a loop." Gregory listened for a while. "Marcus is taking care of me. Listen, he has something he wants to ask you." Gregory handed him the phone, and Marcus took it tentatively. "Ask her, I bet she'd help," Gregory whispered, and Marcus shook his head, but Gregory nodded emphatically.

"Hello, Katherine," Marcus began.

"What do you need to ask me? And why is Gregory calling to soften me up?" She sounded amused rather than upset.

Marcus glared at Gregory, who motioned him to continue. "Angie has to have surgery and she's going to be out for a month or so. I need someone who can help in the store during the day. Would you know someone?" Marcus asked, and Gregory shook his head. "What?" Marcus asked Gregory, moving the phone away from his mouth.

"Ask her. She'll be great with the customers. She wants you to help with her benefit, so ask her to help you in the store while Angie's gone." Gregory sighed at the end of his sentence.

"Sorry," Marcus said into the phone. "I meant, I was wondering if you'd be willing to help out in the store." Marcus waited, not knowing what to expect, but what he heard was a squeal of delight.

"You're serious?" she asked.

"It would be for a few weeks, and then if business keeps picking up, part time after that," Marcus explained, a bit surprised at her reaction.

"I'd love to," she told him. "I informed the school that I wouldn't be volunteering for them anymore, so I definitely have the time."

Marcus smiled brightly. "Then come in, in the morning, and you can work with Angie. She can show you what to do and how to help the customers. Is eight o'clock okay?"

"Perfect," she said. They talked for a few more minutes about what she should wear and where she should park when she came in before hanging up. Marcus could hardly believe it. He actually felt lighter than he had in days.

"You're brilliant, sweetheart," Marcus said, squeezing Gregory's hand. "What made you think of her? Because I never would have."

Gregory rested back on the bed, closing his eyes. "I've told you before. You don't need to do this alone. Katherine cares for you a great deal and she'll do anything she can to help you. I bet your father would too, if you asked him." Somehow Marcus doubted that, but he didn't argue. "You're surrounded by people who care for you and support you, but you don't see it. All you want to do is keep everything close to the vest and take it all on yourself. You don't have to. Katherine wanted you to help with her benefit. It only stood to reason that she should help you in return." Gregory tugged on Marcus's hand until it rested over Gregory's heart. "I'm not the only person who loves you. I know you feel alone a lot, but you're not. Angie loves you, Katherine loves you, Becky idolizes you, and I bet that maybe, under his tank-like exterior, The General loves you too." This time Marcus couldn't help a snort of derision. Gregory didn't argue with him. Instead, he reached up to turn off the light. "Are you going to stay awhile?" Gregory whispered plaintively, and Marcus settled into the chair, leaned his head back, and closed his own eyes. It wasn't long before he heard Gregory's soft breathing, and then before he knew it, he'd dozed off as well.

A nurse coming in to check on Gregory woke him, and Marcus checked the clock before standing up to stretch his back. "He's doing fine," the nurse said as she quietly moved around the room. Gregory barely woke as she checked his vitals and listened to his lungs and heartbeat.

"I'm going to go home," Marcus told Gregory, and he nodded slowly, still mostly asleep. "I'll see you in the morning."

"Get some sleep," Gregory told him, still squeezing his hand. Marcus left the room as quietly as he could before heading down to his car. He barely remembered making the ride home, but as soon as he was in his apartment and in bed, he was wide awake and desperately missed having Gregory sleeping next to him. Thankfully, he didn't stay that way for long, as supreme exhaustion took over and he fell into a deep, if lonely, sleep.

CHAPTER NINE

"I'LL be fine," Gregory said as he got out of bed and walked slowly toward the bathroom. "The doctor said I could go back to work, and that's what I intend to do." It had been a week since he'd been rushed to the hospital, and he was feeling better and much stronger.

"If you don't feel up to it, go home instead of coming to the bakery," Marcus told him, and Gregory snorted.

"Why would I keep away from the best part of my day?" Gregory shook his head as he started getting dressed. "I promise I'll take it easy. Besides, I've been in bed for almost a week, and every time I try to get out, you mother-hen me back in. I'm bored and going stir-crazy."

Marcus stepped closer, and Gregory got a real good whiff of his scent: clean, rich, and musky with overtones of soap. "You have to promise me you'll call if you get too tired. I'll come pick you up."

"Are you going to write a note to get me out of gym class too?" Gregory quipped, and Marcus tugged him closer, kissing him, probably to shut him up, but Gregory didn't mind in the least, especially when Marcus cupped his bare butt cheeks. "Okay, I promise."

"Good," Marcus said before kissing him again. "Is Susan picking you up here?"

"Yes. I called her last night. She seemed really pleased I was staying with you instead of being alone. She's really gruff, but she's kind of nice when you get to know her, especially when I'm her carrot cake and cinnamon roll connection." Gregory smiled brightly as he continued into the bathroom, where he cleaned up, and then he returned to the bedroom to get dressed. Marcus was waiting for him, dressed and ready to go into the bakery.

"I'll see you tonight," Marcus told him, leaning in for a kiss before hurrying out of the apartment. Gregory listened to his footsteps on the stairs before getting ready for work. He knew it was still early and he could have stayed in bed for a while yet, but since he'd met Marcus, his schedule had slowly shifted to that of an extremely early riser. So instead, he watched a little television, unintentionally dozing on the sofa until it was time for Susan to pick him up.

As he left the apartment, he saw her pull up, and he got into the car. "How are you feeling?" Susan asked right away, before pulling away from the curb.

"I'm doing well. Between the doctor and Marcus, I have barely been out of bed in a week, and not in a nice way. How are things with Kate?" he asked, continuing one of their usual topics of conversation.

"Well, I think the vegan thing is history, thank God. She's decided that we can eat foods where the animals aren't killed, so I guess we're just vegetarians now." Susan turned onto the main road, and Gregory saw she was actually smiling.

"How did you change her mind?" Gregory asked, and Susan got an almost evil look in her eye.

"I told her I'd had enough of this vegan stuff and brought home a piece of Marcus's carrot cake and ate it in front of her. I knew I had her when she licked her lips at the spicy scent, but when I let her suck a bit of icing off my finger… uh, well, let's just say we had fun with food, and I actually get to eat again." Susan was actually laughing, something Gregory had rarely seen her do. They talked about nothing of consequence the rest of the way to work. Before they went inside, Susan hugged him quickly. "I'm glad you're back," she told him before walking into the building, leaving Gregory feeling a bit stunned, in a really pleased sort of way. Smiling to himself, he entered the building and went to his desk.

His morning was quiet, with most people stopping by briefly to make sure he was okay. In the afternoon, he got a few assignments from his boss, but almost everyone seemed to watch out for him, and by the end of the day he'd done nothing more strenuous than walk to the bathroom. When he left the office with Susan, she agreed to drop him off at the bakery, but Gregory knew she wasn't going to simply leave. She had that "I want cake" look in her eyes.

Susan parked in front of the bakery. Gregory went inside and found Marcus in the kitchen. "Are you still feeling okay?" Marcus asked as he set his pastry bag aside.

"I'm fine. Better now that I'm here." Gregory leaned in for a quick kiss before letting Marcus get back to work. "I'll relieve Angie so she can get going," he added, setting his things by the desk before he headed back out to the store. "Isn't today Angie's last day?"

"Tomorrow," Marcus answered, "and it looks like Katherine is going to work out really well." Marcus went back to work, and Gregory walked back into the store.

"It's good to have you back," Angie said, and Gregory hugged her.

"It's good to be back, and you hurry up and get well. All of us are going to miss you something terrible," Gregory told her honestly. "Now go on home and spend time with your family," Gregory said with a smile, and Angie reached up and stroked his cheek.

"You and Marcus are part of my family." She let her hand slip away, and Gregory smiled, deeply touched by her kindness. "I'll see both of you tomorrow." Angie left the store, and Gregory found himself alone. He checked everything over as customers came and left. When the store was quiet, he went in the back to see what else was available to fill the cases. He heard the bell just as he stepped into the kitchen, so he rushed back out and found himself face to face with his mother.

Gregory didn't know what to say at first. "Hi, Mom," was all that came out. "I didn't expect to see you again after the other day."

"Greggy," she breathed softly, and he saw tears stream out of her eyes. "I had to come back and see you." She made no move to step forward, and Gregory didn't know what to do.

"Does Dad know you're here?" Gregory asked, and his mother shook her head.

"I've missed you," she said, swallowing hard and finally taking a tentative step forward. Gregory wasn't quite sure how he should react, so he let her make the first move. "There hasn't been a single day that I haven't thought about you." It looked like she might hug him, but she backed away as other customers came in the store, and Gregory went behind the counter, helping the customers before ringing up the sales, until he was once again alone with his mother.

"Why did you leave the other day without saying anything?" Gregory asked, still hurt by the snub, not that he wanted her to know that.

"I was surprised and didn't know what to think. Your father had told me you'd moved away some time ago." She swallowed again. "I never expected to see you again." She stepped toward him, and before Gregory could react, he was being hugged tightly. The surprise took a few seconds to wear off, and then he hugged her too, listening as she cried softly against his bakery apron.

"I didn't think you wanted to see me again," Gregory told her softly, barely able to form the words around the lump in his throat. His mother was holding him. "You never went against what Dad wanted. Why are you doing it now?"

Gregory waited and watched as she stepped back slightly. "I thought it was my duty as a good wife to do what my husband expected, and when he and your uncle said you were evil and possessed by the devil, I believed him. I know now that isn't true.

You're still my son, my little baby, and I don't care what your father says." She was trembling, and Gregory knew no matter what she was saying, his mother still didn't feel comfortable defying Gregory's father.

"And you're still my mother. I've never stopped thinking or caring about you, no matter what he told you," Gregory assured her.

"Your father said you were sick," his mother whispered, touching his cheek lightly.

"I was, when Dad turned his back on me. But I had good friends who took me in and helped me get better."

"So you're all well?" she asked, blinking a few times as tears flowed down her cheeks.

"The disease is under control," Gregory explained. "I'll never be cured, and this is something I'll live with for the rest of my life." Gregory looked at the kitchen doorway as Marcus entered the store.

"Can I help you?" Marcus asked, looking at Gregory's mother.

"Marcus," Gregory said, moving closer to his lover. "This is my mother." Gregory had never expected and barely allowed himself to hope that he'd ever be able to introduce Marcus to his mother. It was almost like some kind of dream.

Marcus extended his hand, but his expression didn't brighten. "It's nice to meet you. Is there something you want?"

"Marcus!" Gregory said, scolding him lightly.

"Your family hasn't had anything to do with you in years. I'm simply being cautious," Marcus explained as his mother opened her worn purse and pulled out a tissue.

"Mom, this is my boyfriend, Marcus. He's also the owner of the bakery," Gregory said as he smiled at Marcus, and he got lost in Marcus's returned smile for a few seconds before turning back to his mother. Gregory saw that she was crying. "What is it?" he asked softly, but she didn't answer and shook her head.

Gregory wondered if she was about to rip into him. When he glanced at Marcus, he got the impression from the concerned look on his face that he thought the same thing. Now Gregory girded himself for another round of self-righteousness from his mother. At least this time Marcus was here with him, and he wouldn't have to face it alone.

"Your son is an amazing man, and if you can't see that, then I suggest you leave and never come back," Marcus said, stepping forward, his arms crossed in front of his chest. "You've hurt him enough, and I won't allow it to happen again in my bakery."

"It's okay, Marcus," Gregory whispered, a little overwhelmed at his support. "She can't hurt me any longer."

"No," Gregory's mother said as the tears continued rolling down her cheeks, the tissue unable to stem the tide. She sniffed and wiped her eyes yet again before reaching into her purse for another tissue. "We were wrong," she said between soft gasps for breath. "Gregory's father and I were wrong. We threw away our son because we weren't willing to accept him for who he was." She gasped one more time, wiping her eyes as she tried to get hold of herself. "After I saw you the other day, I realized what we'd done and that I'd been given a second chance." Gregory stepped forward and hugged her. "I missed my baby." His mother openly sobbed against his chest, and Gregory couldn't help the tears that welled up in his eyes.

"I missed you too," Gregory gasped around his own tears. He was holding his mother in his arms. "I never thought I'd see you again." Gregory didn't say much after that. He simply let go of his feelings. If this was a dream, he didn't want to wake up. For a long time, they held each other. Eventually, Gregory released his mother and stepped back. They looked at each other, and neither of them seemed to know what to say.

"Are you happy?" his mother asked after a long, rather uncomfortable silence.

"Yes," Gregory answered, once again moving closer to Marcus. "I'm very happy. I wasn't for quite a while, but I have a good life, friends who care about me, and someone who loves me for me."

Gregory wanted to kiss Marcus, but decided not to push it. "I know you don't really understand about me being gay, and I know it's hard, but I love you for making the effort."

His mother nodded and sniffed again before stepping toward the door. "I'll stop in again, if that's okay?"

"Of course, Mom," Gregory told her, feeling Marcus take his hand. He stood still, watching her until she'd closed the door and passed in front of the windows. "I never expected to see her again."

"I know." Marcus put his arm around Gregory's waist, squeezing him slightly for a few seconds until the front door opened. Marcus moved away and back into the kitchen while Gregory stepped back behind the counter to help the customers.

He helped a few of the regular customers with their purchases, and the store finally slowed down. Gregory was checking the cases when he heard the bell ring, so he walked back behind the counter. An older woman walked cautiously inside, looking all around. She scowled, and it almost appeared like she'd just tasted something bad. "Can I help you?"

The woman turned to him, and Gregory shivered at the look of hatred in her eyes. "You should be ashamed of yourselves. Promoting sinful behavior with your AIDS benefit. Don't you know that disease is God's punishment for their sins?" Gregory hoped to God Marcus couldn't hear this, but as he moved from behind the counter, he bumped into Marcus, who was as white as a sheet.

"It's my father's prediction come true," Marcus said softly, and Gregory hurried past him.

"HIV is a disease—nothing more," Gregory said as calmly as he could. "I suggest you leave now."

"I'll be sure to tell all my friends to stay away from this place," she spat out as she walked toward the door.

"Since when is it a sin to help children?" Gregory called after her as she opened the door. "I suggest you read your Bible more closely." The door closed, and Gregory glared at her through the glass until she was gone.

His next thought was to find Marcus, but he heard the bell again and found himself standing face to face with Thom. Great, just what he needed.

"Just go away, Thom," Gregory said, turning toward the kitchen door.

"Gregory, please. I'm sorry about what happened, but I really do miss you," Thom said, and Gregory ignored him, trying to angle himself so he could see Marcus. He stepped away from the counter to the kitchen door as Thom grabbed him. Suddenly he was being kissed, Thom taking possession the way he'd always done. Before Marcus, Gregory's brain seemed to switch off when Thom kissed him, but now he realized just how pathetic Thom was, and how stupid he'd been for falling for it time and time again. The scent and taste that he used to crave now seemed stale and dull.

Pulling away, Gregory stared at Thom as he heard a door slam in the back of the kitchen. Without thinking, Gregory drew back his hand and then punched Thom in the jaw. "What in the hell made you think I wanted that?" Gregory yelled as Thom placed his hands over his face, probably for protection. "I've told you to leave me alone."

"Ow," Thom whined like a little child.

"Stop your bellyaching. You had it coming and you know it." Gregory needed to find Marcus.

"Jesus," Thom groaned as he rubbed his jaw. "You didn't have to hit me."

"Talking didn't work, you ass." Gregory stepped back and checked Thom's jaw. "Now go away and leave me alone! Do you understand that now? Find someone else's life to ruin."

"I thought you were playing hard to get," Thom said, a thin trickle of blood running down his lip.

"I wasn't. And so help me God, if you hurt Marcus, I'll hunt you down and cut off your puny little balls!"

Gregory heard the back door again, and he could only hope it was Marcus returning. "And, by the way, Sebastian is on the lookout for you, and he's married to a judge, so I suggest you make yourself scarce before you lose your entire set of family jewels."

"God, what happened to you?" Thom asked. "You used to be so much fun."

"Yeah, I was everyone's good time." Gregory wanted to push Thom out the door. "But some of us grow up when we find out we're HIV positive and nearly die. I grew up and found someone much better than you. Marcus loves me, and I adore him to pieces. So, no, I'm not interested in anything from you, except maybe seeing you on the other side of the door." Gregory glared at Thom, and he finally seemed to get the idea and actually moved toward the door.

Gregory helped the customer who came in as Thom was leaving, and then, once the store was empty, he went in back to find Marcus. What he found instead was an awful mess. One of Marcus's cakes was on the floor in pieces, having fallen from the table, and frosting footsteps led toward the back door. "Marcus," Gregory called tentatively, and he heard movement in the mop closet. "Marcus," Gregory called again, walking closer. He found Marcus wrestling with the wringer. "I take it you saw what happened?"

"If you mean kissing that other man, then, yes, I saw it." Marcus dropped the wringer on the floor with a crash. "I knew something like this was going to happen. Everything has been going too well, and it had to fall apart. My customers won't come in because of the benefit, and you… you were kissing someone else."

Gregory reached out and touched Marcus's shoulder, but he jerked away. "Thom is an ex, and he kissed me—without permission, I might add. And afterwards, I slugged him and split his lip."

"You did?"

"Yes—no one but you gets to kiss me," Gregory explained, and he saw much of the tension drain from Marcus's body.

"He kissed you?"

"Yes, he did, but I didn't want him to, and I punched him. He deserved it too. He's been pestering me for a while now, and I thought he'd give up." Gregory snickered. "Well, he will now."

A ghost of a smile crossed Marcus's lips. "It hurt when I saw you… and him."

"I know, but even when he was kissing me, all I was thinking about was you." Gregory pulled Marcus to him, hugging him with everything he had. "I promise to tell you all about Thom, if you want, but he isn't important. You are, and as for that woman, she was a bitter old hag." Gregory checked the clock, then guided them out toward the store. "I'm sorry you were hurt. I never wanted that to happen… ever."

The bell sounded, and Gregory went out front, with Marcus following behind. "Thom—what do you want?" Gregory asked, and he heard Marcus growl softly from behind him. Gregory smiled, raising his eyebrows.

"I'm sorry," Thom said, before turning and leaving once again.

"So am I," Gregory agreed as the door closed behind Thom. He turned to face Marcus. "Can you forgive me?"

Marcus sighed. "Can you forgive me?"

Gregory nodded. "How about we clean up the mess and get out of here? When we get home, we can have really great 'I'm sorry' sex."

Marcus chuckled and agreed, leaving the front of the store, and they got ready to close.

THEY left the store together, Gregory holding Marcus's hand tightly in his. "Thom was my huge mistake," he began as they walked. "Sebastian and I had had a fight, and I was being stupid."

Marcus squeezed his hand. "You don't need to do this if you don't want to."

"No," Gregory retorted, "you need to know this. It's my own fault. Thom is the reason I screwed up my relationship with Sebastian. He had this hold on me somehow. I can't explain it, but whenever I was near him, it was like my brain would shut off. Anyway, Thom left town, and I thought I was over him, but he showed up again a month or so ago, and it felt the same again. I hated it and ignored it, because you are more important to me than he is." Gregory stared straight ahead as he continued.

"Is that what you felt when he kissed you?" Marcus asked with a hint of jealousy.

"No. See, that's the amazing thing—I felt nothing. It was like kissing a stranger, and that's because of you. I don't want anyone but you."

Marcus stopped walking for a few seconds, gazing at Gregory before continuing. "You're serious?"

"Of course I am. You're the best thing to ever happen to me." Gregory kissed Marcus's hand as they passed under one of the trees that lined the sidewalk. They turned from Hanover Street onto Pomfret Street and continued walking.

"I have something I want to ask you," Marcus told him. "The lease on my place is up in a few months, and it's rather small. I was thinking of looking for a larger place, and I was wondering if you'd come with me."

"Of course," Gregory answered, "but you don't need me to choose an apartment for you."

Marcus moved a little closer. "I sort of thought that if we found an apartment we both liked...." Marcus let his words fall off, and Gregory got the message.

"You want to get an apartment together?"

"Well, yes," Marcus said, and Gregory turned to him with a huge grin.

"You really want me to live with you?" He could hardly believe it after what had happened over the past few hours.

Marcus nodded and smiled. "Of course I do. I love you." They stopped walking, and Marcus turned toward him. "When you got ill, I honestly thought I might lose you. I never want to feel that way again, and I don't want to wait around for something else to happen. I know it may be a little fast, and if you want to wait, that's okay."

Gregory cut off Marcus's words by kissing him right there on the sidewalk. "I want to be with you too. More than anything."

"I thought that maybe together we could get an apartment large enough for the two of us. Sebastian knows a lot of people, and I suspect he can help us find something we'd like." Both of their apartments were really small, but together they could get something with a little more room. "How much time do you have on your lease?" Marcus asked as they began walking again.

"I'm month to month, so I just have to give thirty days' notice," Gregory explained, holding Marcus's hand. "Do you think we can get a place with maybe a yard or a small balcony?"

"We can look for anything you like," Marcus told him with an excited smile. "I want you to be happy." Marcus squeezed his hand as they continued. "So, to change the subject. You've had a little while to think about it. How do you feel about your mother showing up at the bakery? I know you felt pretty rejected when she left the last time without saying anything."

"I don't know," Gregory answered as honestly as his conflicted heart and mind would allow. "I want to jump up and down that she came by and I was able to talk to her. And I really want to hope that what she told me was the truth, but I'm not sure if I can believe her."

"Why?" Marcus asked, and Gregory appreciated the concern he heard in his voice.

"When my father cut me off, I knew my mother felt differently than he did. I could see it in her eyes the last time I saw her, but she said nothing. She won't stand up to my father, so if he finds out she came to see me and forbids her from coming again, she won't." They turned the corner a block away from Marcus's apartment, the cobblestone sidewalk uneven under their feet. Gregory stumbled slightly, and Marcus caught him, holding him up. "I don't doubt that the way she feels is what she said, because I've never known her to lie, but she won't stand up for herself or for me." Gregory desperately wished that she would, but that was something he'd never seen when he was growing up, and he didn't think she was capable of changing now.

"At least you got to see her," Marcus reminded him, and Gregory nodded his agreement.

"Yes. And at least I know she cares," Gregory said with a dry throat. "I don't know if I'll see her again or not, but no matter what, I'll know my mother loves me. She may not feel as though she can tell my father, but at least I know she does love me, and I can live with that. My family hasn't been a part of my life for a while," Gregory explained as they continued walking the last little way to Marcus's apartment. "But now I know part of my family still cares for me."

"Even if they won't stand up for you?" Marcus asked, and Gregory shrugged.

"They're not as important as other people in my life, the ones I have no doubt will stand up for me." Gregory bumped Marcus's shoulder as they approached Marcus's building. "And since we're speaking of families, what about yours?"

Marcus unlocked the door, and they climbed the stairs. "I haven't heard anything more from The General, which is good. Let him bother my stepbrothers and sisters with his advice," Marcus told him happily. "Katherine is still trying to do what she can to get us to talk to each other. I know she means well, but I'm starting to think of that as a lost cause. He is the way he is and that's not going to change."

"And neither are you," Gregory told him with a chuckle. "You know, you're just like him, and that's why you don't get along." Marcus turned to him indignantly, and Gregory laughed even harder.

"I am not," Marcus countered without heat.

"You are too. Marcus Wilson, I love you more than anyone I've ever met, but you are just like your father," Gregory pressed, and Marcus whirled around, his eyes blazing. "You even look like him when you're angry." Gregory leaned against the banister in the stairway, his arms crossed in front of his chest.

"I am definitely not my father," Marcus stated.

"No, you aren't. But, like your father, you need to be in control, and you're just as stubborn as he is. Those aren't bad qualities, necessarily, but it means that the two of you don't get along." Gregory followed Marcus as he stomped up the stairs to the apartment door, and he couldn't help laughing as Marcus proved his point for him. "Come on, Marcus, I wasn't trying to make you angry. I just want you to see the reason you don't get along with your dad. In some ways, I'm very like my own father. I don't listen to others sometimes, and I can be just as stubborn and closed-minded as he is."

"I've never known you to be closed-minded," Marcus said as he set his keys on the kitchen counter.

"I used to be," Gregory admitted. "I thought I knew best and that I could do whatever I wanted. It took me a while to realize that I behaved the way I did when I was with Sebastian because I was acting like my father. He figures he can do no wrong, and I thought the same thing, that whatever I did was right because it was what I wanted. That cost me Sebastian and my health. But I learned from it, I hope, and I'd do everything all over again because it brought me to you. My successes, as well as my mistakes, all brought me to you."

"So what do you want me to do, obey his every order?" Marcus asked, and Gregory smiled.

"No. Just be yourself and let your dad see that. Let him see the man I love, the one who works hard and is willing to sacrifice himself to help others." Gregory pulled Marcus into his arms. "He'll see what an incredible, wonderful, and loving son he raised, and then he can't help being proud of you."

Marcus held him tightly, and Gregory felt him begin to shake. "You know it doesn't matter what I do. My father rarely sees anything I've ever done as worthwhile." Gregory held Marcus, and it took him a second before he realized his lover was crying. "I feel like such a doofus for going to pieces on you like this." Marcus wiped his eyes with his hands.

"You're allowed, after what happened today," Gregory said, hugging Marcus again. "I didn't mean to make you feel this way about anything. Honest."

Marcus held him for a long while before they made dinner together in Marcus's cramped kitchen and then went to bed. Gregory figured his mother showing up at the store was a gift he'd never expected to get, and he wondered how Marcus could get the same thing from his father. An exhausted Marcus fell right to sleep, and Gregory held him tight, thanking all the gods that he hadn't messed everything up… like before.

CHAPTER TEN

THE past two weeks had been good and quiet, Marcus thought as he yawned and got out of bed. He kept expecting that to change, but so far it hadn't. It was a Sunday morning, and he had plenty of work to do. The benefit for Reggie was in three days, and he had to make dessert for a thousand people. He'd promised Katherine that he would do it, and he wasn't going to disappoint her. She'd been working her butt off at the bakery for weeks, and while no one could replace Angie, Katherine was doing her very best and coming close. She'd also come through in a big way in that she'd found donors for most of the major ingredients, so Marcus woke up early on his only day off and left Gregory still sleeping as he walked over the cool wooden floors to the bathroom. He was definitely a bit bleary-eyed as he cleaned up and took care of business. When he was done, he turned off the light and quietly walked out of the bathroom, trying not to disturb Gregory.

"What time is it?"

Marcus leaned over the bed, kissing Gregory on the cheek. "It's six o'clock."

"Then what are you doing up? It's Sunday," Gregory whined as he tugged Marcus back toward the bed.

"I have to go in to the bakery. The benefit is Wednesday, and I need to get the dessert finished. Today is my only chance to do it."

Marcus yawned, doing his best to stifle it. "I have to get the last cake layers baked and let them cool fully before I can finish the cakes, so if I don't get started now, I'll be working until late tonight." Marcus kissed Gregory once again. "Go back to sleep for a while."

"Is there anything I can do to help?"

"Later, if you want," Marcus said, and after Gregory kissed him again, he rolled over and went back to sleep. Marcus got dressed as quietly as he could and left the apartment, hurrying to his car. Normally, he'd walk to the bakery, but time was of the essence, so he drove and parked, then turned on the lights as he entered the building.

Marcus closed and locked the door behind him before turning on the ovens and getting to work mixing the cake batter. He'd already taken the time to figure up the amount he needed, so he got right to work measuring ingredients into the large mixer. Then he prepared the pans and got the first set of layers into the oven. He didn't have enough oven space to bake everything at once, so while the first batch was baking, Marcus cleaned the mixing bowl and started preparing the second batch of batter. By the time the first set of layers was ready to come out of the oven, he had the pans greased, filled, and ready to take their place.

He'd just shut the oven door when he heard a knock at the front door. Leaving the kitchen, he went to open it and saw Gregory standing out front, with his stepmother and Maureen right behind him. "What are all of you doing here?"

"Gregory called and said you were baking for the benefit," Maureen explained as she stepped inside. "I told you I would help," she scolded as he closed the door and went to lock it.

"I'll get it," Katherine said, and Marcus motioned Maureen and Gregory toward the kitchen.

"So where are you?" Maureen asked, taking off her jacket and then pulling on one of her work aprons before passing her hand over one of the cooling layers. "I can get these out of the pans if you want."

"Okay, thank you," Marcus replied, feeling a bit overwhelmed. He hadn't expected all this help. "I was about to start on the dishes before mixing the frosting."

Gregory began gathering the dirty pans and taking them to the sink, and once the large mixing bowl was clean, Marcus started weighing out the ingredients for the buttercream. "What can we do?" Katherine said from the doorway, and Marcus looked up to see her and, to his surprise, The General, who was carrying a take-out container of coffee.

"Dad," Marcus said, hardly believing his eyes. "I wasn't expecting you."

He stepped forward and set the coffee on the counter. "I brought enough for everyone," he said, and Maureen took a cup, thanking him before returning to her work. "Can't start the day without strong coffee," he explained before walking over to where Marcus was standing, still a bit stunned. "I've spent plenty of time on KP, so I thought I'd come down and help." The General looked around the kitchen. "You know, we could set this up like a production line and…."

Marcus should have known that as soon as his father set foot in his kitchen, he'd try to take over. "Dad," Marcus said levelly. "What sort of skills do you have? Can you ice a cake so it's perfectly level and uniform, every single time? Or stack and fill cake layers so the cake is perfectly level and flat?"

"Well," his father began, and Marcus saw Katherine step up behind him and say something into his ear.

Marcus had to work to keep his temper under control. Part of him wanted to ask his father to simply leave, but he'd come down here to help, probably at Katherine's urging, and making quips at him wasn't going to help at all.

"Katherine, I'm going to have you work with Maureen as her assistant. You'll get things for her and help her any way you can." Katherine and Maureen had instantly gotten along, so he figured them working together would be a good fit. Katherine joined her compatriot with a smile. Maureen continued removing the layers from the pans, then placed them in the refrigerator to fully cool. "I'm going to have the two of you work on the three-tiered cake for Reggie. Katherine knows him, so I want it to be a cake Reggie would love. The square layers are for that cake, and I want the two of you to have fun with it. Gregory and I are going to work on the side cakes that will make up the bulk of the dessert for the benefit. The layers in the oven are to replace the cake layers for the store, so all we need to do is cool them and put them away." Marcus saw smiling faces shining back at him. "So let's make some cake."

Maureen and Katherine got to work, the two of them putting their heads together, talking over ideas while Maureen finished getting the layers in to cool. He knew she'd use all the older store layers before the ones he'd just baked both to turn the stock and because cold cake was much easier to work with.

"Do you want me to finish the dishes?" Gregory asked.

"Please. I need to talk to my father for a few minutes," Marcus said, glancing to where The General stood, watching the activity. Gregory nodded, and Marcus kissed him lightly before walking to where his father seemed to be waiting for him. "Let's go out into the store," Marcus said, gesturing to his dad. "Thank you for coming to help," he said once they were away from the others. "It was a bit of a surprise." *To say the very least.*

His father looked uncomfortable. "You really know what you're doing," he finally said. "You have a plan and you're executing it with precision."

"This is what I do, Dad. The bakery is going to be a success because of me and all those who've supported me." Marcus took a deep breath and released it slowly. "A lot of the reason for that success is the training I had in doing things right the first time and doing everything as efficiently as possible. Does that sound familiar?" His father nodded. "I learned a lot of that from you." Marcus felt emotion welling up from his chest, and he tried to keep it under control. "I know what I'm doing and I'm good at it. I know I'm not the son you would have asked for and that I've disappointed you in so many ways, but I am who I am, and I work hard. I would think that should be enough to have earned some degree of respect from you, if nothing else."

Marcus waited for some sort of response from his father. He expected either an argument or at the very least some sort of list of the ways he'd disappointed him. What he didn't expect was what actually happened. His father, The General, stepped forward and pulled him into a hug that nearly drove the breath from his lungs.

"You have never been a disappointment to me or your mother. You're my son, and I have always loved you." Marcus heard his dad's voice break, something he couldn't ever remember happening before. "Talking about my feelings has never been my strong suit. I didn't get to where I was in the service by having feelings or catering to those of other people, and sometimes I forget to tell the ones I care about how I feel." His father released him, and Marcus stepped back, a lot surprised and a bit manhandled. For the first time in a while, Marcus saw real emotion on his father's face—well, other than anger or what he'd always thought of as indifference where he was concerned. His father swallowed hard and shook his head slightly before the expression Marcus was used to slid back into place, and in that second, Marcus realized what he'd been seeing all these years from his father was a mask. He'd gotten a glimpse of the man underneath, someone whom only Katherine got to see on a regular basis.

"You know, Dad, you don't have to be The General around me. Because all I ever wanted from you was for you to just be my dad." Marcus wiped his eyes, not caring if his father saw how he felt. "I don't want to be commanded or talked at, but talked to, and asked my opinion. I'm an adult, the child you helped raise, and you did a good job."

His father nodded, and Marcus figured he'd gotten more than he'd ever hoped for from his dad, so he turned to go back to work.

"If I did a good job, then why are you… gay?"

Marcus whirled around. The idea that his father would somehow blame himself had never occurred to him. "You didn't do anything, and neither did Mom. I'm gay because I was born that way." Now it was his turn to hug his father. "You raised me well and taught me the value of hard work and going after your dreams. Mine just aren't the same as yours, but that doesn't mean I didn't learn the lesson." He felt his father's arms close around him once again, this time much more gently. "I love you too, Dad," Marcus whispered, and then his father released him. He didn't have any illusions that all their problems were solved, but it was a great start, and maybe they could grow to understand one another.

"So," his father began as they walked back toward the kitchen, "what do you need me to do?"

"Well," Marcus said with a grin, "it looks like you pulled dish duty." He half expected his father to protest, but he didn't. Instead, he walked to the sink, where Gregory was working, and took over for him. Gregory washed his hands and then pulled on gloves before joining Marcus at the workstation.

He and Gregory fell into a routine, and Marcus was able to teach Gregory some basic skills. It wasn't long before Gregory was doing things like spreading the filling and whipping the buttercream to the correct consistency. The work took until the early afternoon, but by the time they were done, Marcus and Gregory had built and frosted twenty-plus plain cakes for service, and the ladies had created a colorful three-tiered cake with a basketball theme. It wasn't frilly or busy, but it was polished and a great example of the work they could do. "Reggie will love it," Marcus told them both as he looked it over. "It's perfect." Marcus helped them move the cake into the cooler. He took one more look around and smiled. "I want to thank all of you for your help. I really appreciate it." Marcus found himself gravitating toward Gregory without giving it much thought, and soon his arm was around his lover's waist.

"It's for a good cause," Maureen told him. She wasn't a big woman, but Maureen had a huge personality, and her praise and help meant a great deal to him. "Now I have to get home, but I'll see you Tuesday." Maureen kissed him on the cheek and then grabbed her things before heading toward the front door. "Marcus!" she screamed, and he took off toward the front of the store.

In the store, he saw Maureen pointing toward the windows, which had been sprayed with what looked like white paint. "They took off toward the square."

"Call the police," Marcus said, racing out the door. On a Sunday there was very little foot traffic on the sidewalks, and he saw two kids, surprisingly young, at a run, turn the corner at the square. He barely got a glimpse, but at least he could tell the police which way they'd gone. Turning around, he headed back toward the bakery as sirens reached his ears and got louder.

Marcus stood outside his bakery reading the word "AIDS" sprayed crudely on the lower portion of his windows. It was obviously kids, and most likely the ones he'd seen. As he stood there, Marcus heard the bakery door open, and Gregory came out and walked over to where he stood. "I'm sorry," Gregory whispered.

"It's not your fault," Marcus muttered. Feeling angry and violated, he stood on the sidewalk shaking from head to toe. The others joined them a few seconds later, and Marcus girded himself for his father to say his "I told you so."

"Goddamned son of a bitching parents can't raise their children for shit!" came out of his father's mouth, followed by a string of curses and sheer anger, the likes of which Marcus had never heard from his father before.

"Can anyone tell us what happened?" a police officer asked, and when The General turned toward him, the police officer did a double take before approaching. "I'm Officer Cloud."

Before he could ask another question, Maureen was off and running. "I saw them. As I was getting ready to leave, I came out through the store and saw them finishing their little missive," Maureen almost spat. "I got a good look at them too. They had to be about twelve or thirteen, in jeans. One was wearing a red T-shirt with a skull on it, and the other green with a cubicle design. Little bastards were pressed up against the glass so they could get as high as they could." Maureen was a great worker and she didn't talk a lot, but get her going and she was like a top and you just had to wait until she wound down before you were going to get a word in.

"They took off toward the square. I saw them running, but didn't chase them. They were too far away. They headed toward Dickinson," Marcus supplied, and the officer radioed in the information. Then he moved closer to the windows and examined the white stuff that continued to run down the panes.

"I don't think it's spray paint," he said, pulling out a tissue and wiping at it. "I'm not sure what it is, but it seems water soluble, so it'll clean off pretty easily." He took all their names and addresses as more chatter came across the radio. "We found them," Officer Cloud said with a smile. "One of the cars is picking them up, and they're going to bring them back over so you can identify them."

"I'd like to smack some sense into both of them," Maureen spat, and Marcus tugged her into a hug, his heart rate finally slowing to something closer to normal.

"It's okay," he told her, "and I promise, if there's going to be any hitting, you get first shot." Maureen's anger vanished in a fit of laughter that seemed contagious.

"If I have to go back into battle, young lady, I'm taking you with me," Marcus's father said with a grin, and Marcus stared, open-mouthed.

"You do have a sense of humor," he quipped to his dad, getting a smile in return. Another police car approached, and two officers got out, followed by two young boys who looked as though this wasn't their first ride in a police car.

"We didn't do anything," the one in the red shirt protested, even thought he had white stuff on his hands. The kid had hair that looked like it hadn't been washed in a week, and Marcus was really pleased he was upwind from him and planned to stay that way. The other one looked a bit cleaner. Obviously both kids had parents who didn't give a damn.

"Then how come you have this on your hands?" the officer said, turning over the kid's hand to show everyone. "Why'd you do it?"

Both boys looked down at the ground.

"Why!" Marcus's father snapped in a tone Marcus knew he'd worked for years to perfect.

"They're the guys helping that AIDS kid," the boy in the green said softly. "One of our teachers in school was talking about him like he was some sort of hero because he got sick and that school wouldn't let him in."

"He's a good kid and he doesn't deserve to be treated that way," Marcus told the kids. "No one does. If it were you in his place, you'd want people to help you." Neither of them had anything to say about that.

"You gonna take us to jail?" the green-shirted kid asked, looking more than a little scared.

"That's up to this man here. It's his windows you messed up, and I'm going to give him a chance to think about it while you're cleaning up the mess you made." The one police officer looked to the other. "Did you take pictures for evidence?"

"Yes," the other officer answered.

"No judge is gonna send us to jail, Bert," the red-shirted kid said, looking a little more defiant.

"Oh yeah?" Gregory said as he stepped forward. "I live next door to a judge, and I can help see to it that he gets your case, and then we'll see how much time you spend in jail. Now get to work." Marcus had never seen Gregory act mean or tough before. It was kind of sexy. Gregory went inside and returned a little later with some rags and window cleaner. "I said get cleaning!" Gregory sounded angry, and Marcus realized this probably wasn't an act; this had probably hurt him. Marcus wanted to get Gregory home and away from this, but they couldn't leave.

The kids made a show of cleaning up the mess they'd made. There was no real harm to the building, but they grumbled and complained about how hot it was the entire time.

"That's enough!" Marcus's father ordered, The General coming out in spades. "You made this mess, so you'll clean it up, and while you're at it, you're going to clean all the windows, the doors, and scrub the sidewalk." The General got into the red T-shirted kid's face. Marcus couldn't hear what he said, but the kid turned white as a sheet and went back to work without so much as another sound.

"I'll go get something to drink," Katherine said, and she walked down the street, returning in a bit with cold sodas. She offered one to each of them and the officers, pointedly ignoring the kids as they worked. Then she took pity on them and gave each of the boys a soda too. People passed by and stopped, asking what happened.

"These kids defaced my son's bakery windows and they're cleaning up their mess."

"Good," the passersby said without further comment and continued on. The General did indeed make them clean the sidewalk to his satisfaction. The concrete probably hadn't looked that good since the day it was poured.

"Do you want to press charges?" one of the officers asked, and Marcus shook his head. "We'll take them home and have a talk with each of their parents." The kids were ushered into the police car and then the door closed. "I'd love to know what you said to them," the police officer said to Marcus's dad. Marcus was wondering what he'd said as well, but wasn't going to ask.

The police cars pulled away, and everyone drifted inside, except Maureen, who was now really late, and she hurried away after giving both him and Gregory hugs. "I'll see you Tuesday."

"She's something else," Marcus's father commented. "I was serious. She would be great in combat." He and Katherine gathered their things and prepared to leave as well. "Bye, son, we'll see you in a week for dinner," The General added, and then Katherine hugged them both. His father shook hands with them before walking toward the door.

"Thanks," Marcus said as they left, and then he closed the door behind them.

"What's got you looking so confused?" Gregory asked as they hurried through the bakery, making sure everything was turned off and put away.

"My dad," Marcus said, and then he burst into a smile.

"I take it you talked," Gregory said.

"Yeah, we did," Marcus walked to where Gregory was waiting for him. "And he didn't say 'I told you so' about the whole window mess." Marcus had expected it after their previous conversations.

"So things are okay?" Gregory asked as he flipped off the kitchen lights and followed Marcus as he made his way toward the door.

Marcus remained quiet as they left the bakery and locked the doors behind them. "I don't know. But I think they'll be better between us, and that's all I can ask for." They got into Marcus's car and drove to his apartment.

"Are you tired?" Gregory asked once they were inside, and Marcus flopped down onto the sofa, motioning for Gregory to sit next to him.

"Maybe a little, but I'm not too tired for you," Marcus told his lover as he tugged him down onto the cushions. They curled together in the cool, air-conditioned room, Marcus's eyes already feeling a bit heavy. Gregory turned on the television, keeping the volume low, and Marcus continued closer to sleep.

"This breaking story coming up at five o'clock: the Martin Derry School has rescinded their previous decision and agreed to admit Reggie Perth. The public outcry was too much for them to ignore. More in an hour."

"She did it," Marcus said, knowing the bulk of the credit went to Katherine.

"We all did it," Gregory said as he curled closer, kissing him softly. "And now that benefit will be a celebration, and everyone will be doing it with your cake."

Marcus chuckled softly, and he felt Gregory's weight shift away from him. "Let's go someplace where we can be more comfortable." Gregory took him by the hand and led him toward the bedroom.

EPILOGUE

"How'D it go?" Marcus asked as Gregory strode into the bakery with Katherine right behind him, both of them grinning like cats.

"Are you kidding?" Katherine said, nearly laughing. "They didn't know what hit them. Dressing Gregory up in a tux with a tray to hand out cake samples was brilliant. Those brides-to-be took one bite and every one of them melted. Then this handsome man of yours led them to our booth like the Pied Piper."

Marcus set down his pastry bag. "So you did well," he said, their enthusiasm contagious.

"Beyond well," Gregory said, handing Marcus a stack of appointment cards. "We booked sixty wedding-cake appointments over the next six weeks for weddings out as far as nine months. And we even sold the cake you made for the booth."

"How did you do that? I thought we were going to use it for samples toward the end of the show," Marcus commented as Gregory placed several hundred-dollar bills in his hand.

"Do you remember that couple you helped when their bakery screwed up their wedding date? Well, apparently that's happened with that bakery more than once, including today, and this couple came to the show to find someone to help them. The bride, Carol, was so thrilled to have a cake, and she fell in love with the one you did for the show, so tomorrow that cake is the star at a real wedding, and we've made another couple very happy." Gregory beamed at him.

"But did you have enough samples?" Marcus asked, looking down at the stack of appointment cards. "I guess you did."

"We used the cake you sent and cut the pieces small. The brides had enough cake samples that all they needed was a bite of your cake and they were hooked." Gregory grinned once again, and Marcus pulled him into a tight hug, nearly lifting Gregory off his feet, and swung him around. Marcus had been very worried that the money he'd spent on the booth for the bridal show wouldn't do any good, but it looked like that worry had been for nothing.

"Things are really coming together," Marcus said, allowing himself to truly believe it for the first time.

"Yes, they are," Katherine said from the other side of the worktable. "And I'm still getting calls from people who attended Reggie's benefit, asking who made the cake."

Marcus had stopped twirling Gregory around, but still felt like dancing through the kitchen. "Have you put together the final numbers from the benefit? Did things come out as well as you thought?" Marcus asked, keeping his arm around Gregory's waist. The benefit a week and a half ago for Reggie had been a huge success. As expected, the benefit had quickly turned into a victory celebration, and the governor had even made a brief appearance, shaking hands and posing for pictures with Reggie and Joanna. It was an election year, after all.

"We raised enough money to cover Reggie's back medical expenses, and once he begins attending school, they agreed to begin covering his current expenses. It seems the school's board had been very apologetic and accommodating, especially when state assembly members and public opinion began turning against them." Katherine sighed softly. "But in a way I'm glad it's over. Those benefits are totally exhausting, and working here at the same time wore me out."

"So once Angie comes back, do you want to stay on?" Marcus asked. He'd seen how tired she'd gotten, but he had been hoping she would want to continue working. The business was growing fast, and more than anything, he needed people he could trust in the store. "I could use you part time, particularly in the afternoons."

"Of course I'll stay. The last month has been great. How is Angie doing?" Katherine asked.

"She'll be back right after the Fourth, and when she called, she sounded like she'd been going stir-crazy," Marcus told her with a chuckle. "I imagine her doctor had to lay down the law or she would have been back to work already." He'd already started receiving a call from her once a day, and she made him tell her everything that was going on. Sometimes Marcus thought he was surrounded by mother hens, but he really didn't mind. "We'll work out a schedule when you come in on Monday. Becky wants to work different hours this summer, so I'm going to have to rework everything regardless."

"That's fine," Katherine agreed. "Will we see you two tomorrow for dinner?"

Marcus looked at Gregory and shook his head. "We have plans for the entire day tomorrow. Can we make it next week?"

"Sure," Katherine said before gathering her things. "I'll see both of you next week." Katherine waved before leaving the kitchen. Marcus heard her speaking with Becky on the way out. After a few seconds, Becky stuck her head into the kitchen. "Does Katherine working here once Grandma comes back mean that I'll be working in the kitchen?"

"Most of the time, yes. I'll still need you to help in the store, but not as much as you are doing now." She seemed pleased. "Go ahead and start closing. It's been quiet for a while, and we can get out of here." Becky agreed, and she hurried away.

"So what are these plans you have for tomorrow?" Gregory whispered as he moved into Marcus's arms.

"Nothing other than spending the day in bed," Marcus told him softly, his voice deepening as his body reacted to the close proximity of his lover. "And I thought maybe in the afternoon we could take a look at a place for the two of us. Sebastian said one of Robert's colleagues has a small house for rent on the south side of town, on a great street. It has two bedrooms and a gorgeous garden with a patio. They're looking to rent it to someone who'll be sure to keep it up."

"And we can see it tomorrow?" Gregory asked. Marcus nodded once before cupping Gregory's cheeks and bringing their mouths together in a searing kiss that left both of them more than a little breathless.

"I'm heading out," Becky called from the front. "You two have fun."

"I'll lock up after her," Gregory said, and Marcus watched him go, his tight butt swinging just a little. Marcus finished the task he'd begun before Katherine and Gregory had returned and placed the cake in the cooler before starting the cleanup process.

Gregory slipped his arms around Marcus's waist as he worked, and within seconds, his mind wasn't on cleaning up any longer. Marcus turned around and kissed Gregory hard, then turned them until Gregory was pressed against the worktable. The kiss continued to deepen, and Marcus lifted Gregory off his feet, pressing him further back.

"We shouldn't do this here," Gregory murmured against his lips, but Marcus was already raring to go, and it took a few seconds for the rational side of his brain to take over again. But he didn't let Gregory up right away, instead gentling the kiss until Gregory slid his arms around his neck. "Not that I wouldn't mind having some fun with food." Gregory kissed him and then slipped back onto his feet. "You finish here, and I'll be right back."

Marcus noticed Gregory adjusting his pants as he walked back toward the small work desk. Tearing his eyes away from his lover, Marcus finished cleaning up. "I'm almost done," Marcus said to Gregory as he passed him, heading toward the front door. He finished wiping down the worktable and set aside the cloth to be washed.

"Good," Gregory said from the doorway. "Oh, and don't forget the pastry bag." Gregory disappeared, leaving Marcus with the image of him licking icing off Gregory's skin. Without thinking, he grabbed one of the small decorator bags out of the refrigerator and took off after him as Gregory's laughter echoed off the kitchen walls.

ANDREW GREY grew up in western Michigan with a father who loved to tell stories and a mother who loved to read them. Since then he has lived throughout the country and traveled throughout the world. He has a master's degree from the University of Wisconsin-Milwaukee and works in information systems for a large corporation. Andrew's hobbies include collecting antiques, gardening, and leaving his dirty dishes anywhere but in the sink (particularly when writing). He considers himself blessed with an accepting family, fantastic friends, and the world's most supportive and loving partner. Andrew currently lives in beautiful historic Carlisle, Pennsylvania.

Visit Andrew's website at http://www.andrewgreybooks.com and blog at http://andrewgreybooks.livejournal.com/.

E-mail him at andrewgrey@comcast.net.

The Taste of Love stories by ANDREW GREY

http://www.dreamspinnerpress.com

Also by ANDREW GREY

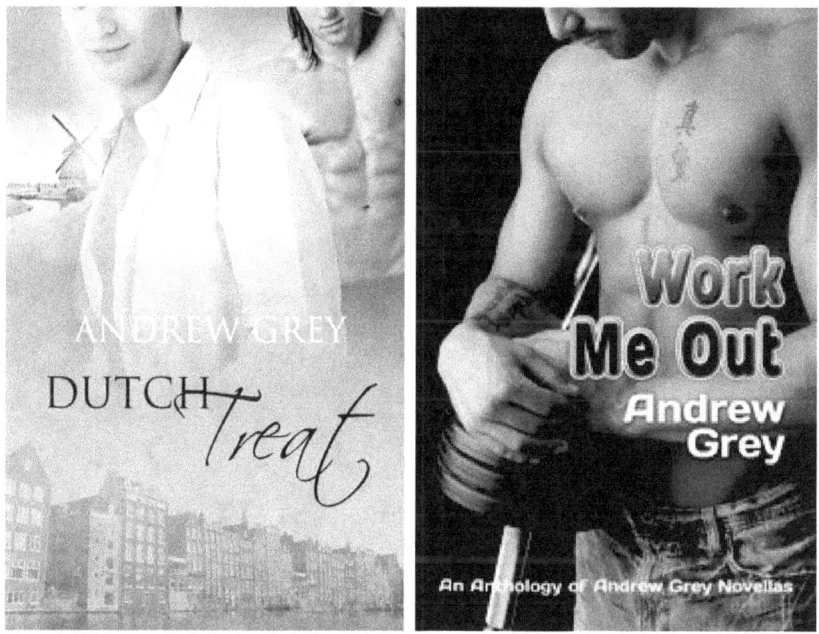

http://www.dreamspinnerpress.com

Golden Rose for Best Contemporary 2011
at Love Romances & More

ACCOMPANIED
by a
Waltz

ANDREW GREY

http://www.dreamspinnerpress.com

The LOVE MEANS… stories

http://www.dreamspinnerpress.com

The CHILDREN OF BACCHUS stories

http://www.dreamspinnerpress.com

The BOTTLED UP stories

http://www.dreamspinnerpress.com

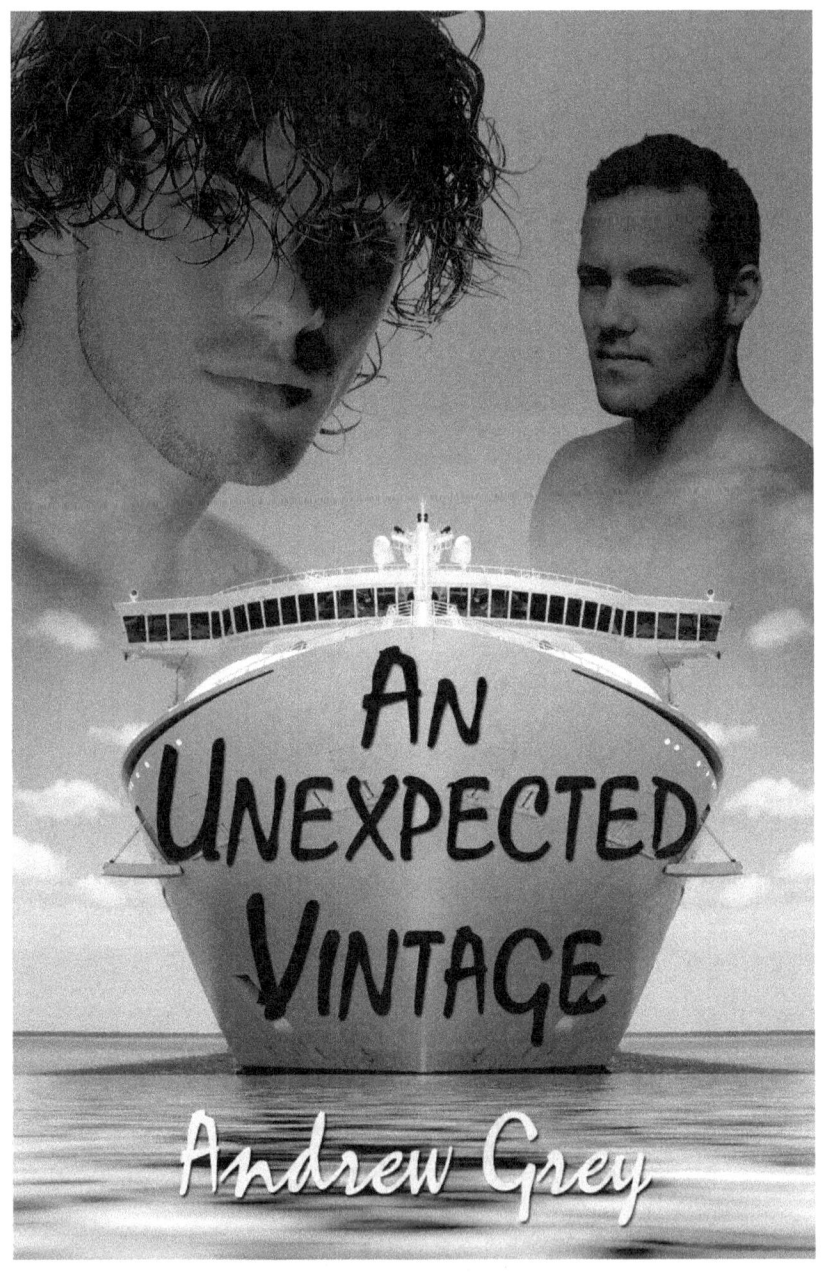

An UNEXPECTED VINTAGE

Andrew Grey

The ART stories

http://www.dreamspinnerpress.com

Also from DREAMSPINNER PRESS

Work Me Out
Andrew Grey

An Anthology of Andrew Grey Novellas

http://www.dreamspinnerpress.com

The RANGE stories

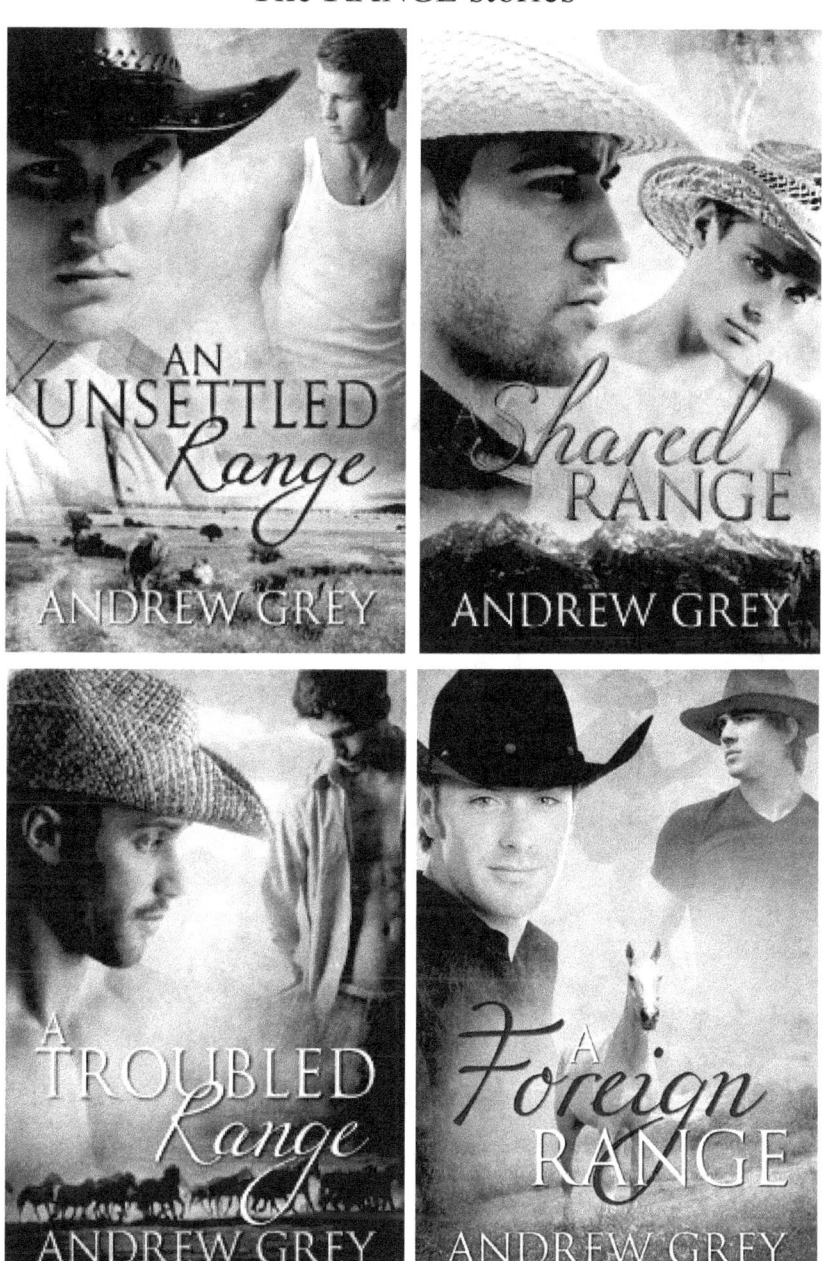

http://www.dreamspinnerpress.com

THREE FATES

ANDREW GREY   MARY CALMES
AMY LANE